for Rosie, Liz & Joy,
with love and admiration

Dear Ceridwen

Dear Ceridwen I

They ring to tell me they are coming, but only after they arrive will tell me what the visit is for. I understand. By now I know all their procedures well enough. I wonder if they think that I am a cold person; I don't cry when they tell me. Only you, Ceridwen, would notice the way my body sets hard along the shoulders, the fogging of my already clouded eyes.

I am carrying up the coffee tray from the kitchen when I hear their feet outside the front door: a woman's, light as Daisy's feline step, and a man's, heavy as the weight of the news he is about to break. Their voices are subdued, talking in whitewashed tones. Defeat sags in their silences like old elastic.

I am relieved that I've had time to tidy before they arrive, not that one person and a cat can make much mess in a three storey building, but the room looks cosy and the fire is lit. I can imagine Nain's approving voice, 'There's nice, Bethan.'

I usher them to the sofa and place steaming coffee cups carefully into their waiting hands. I spoon sugar into their cups, the only comfort I can offer, and settle into the armchair to hold myself together to hear their news. You are there in my mind's eye, Ceridwen: the way your dark hair escapes in riots of curls from a scarlet band, the scuffing on your familiar brown suede boots, more vivid than these strangers seated in my living room.

Across the room the policeman leans forward uncomfortably, longing to have already left. The woman sips coffee, clears her throat and brushes back a strand of dark hair. Her eyes are red-rimmed, as though she has stood too close to a bonfire, so I know that she will be the one to tell me.

After they leave I sit for a long time in the arm chair hardly moving, hardly breathing. When I stir, the December sky outside is darkening and I realise I'm cold; the fire has died down to almost nothing. I shiver and shake myself.

"You've been hours in this chair, girl," I say out loud.

I feel stiff when I stand to pull the heavy plum velvet curtain behind the armchair to blot out the darkness. I force myself to go to the coal tunnel, scuttle in hand.

Back upstairs I riddle the ash through the stove's grate. Fat tears begin to fall as I drop the plump coals onto the flaming fire lighters. I sit in front of the stove while the fire catches. It begins to blaze behind the smoky glass and I rock till the guttural wails slowly subside into sobs.

'There now, Bethan, you wipe your eyes, cariad. A hot bath and a plate of hot toast is what you need.'

"If only that would do the trick, Nain," I reply, as though it's normal to hear the dead.

'Don't you worry about doing the trick. It won't happen all at once, cariad. One day at a time will do you. Come to think of it, an hour at a time'll do. It's not like she's dead now.' Nain's soothing tone shifts to her hands-on-hips voice, brisk as an egg whisk, 'So, which is it to be first, Bethan-girl, bath or food?'

"Bath."

I always think of Nain as being with me, Ceridwen. I imagine what she would say constantly, but this is the first time I actually hear her voice. I haul myself upstairs to the bathroom. Nain is quiet now; faded back into my head, I tell myself, but I cling to the words as though they are as real as the hot water tumbling into the blue enamel bath. *It's not like she's dead now.*

A sudden idea comes to me. I leave the water running onto a crumbled orange bath bar, bubbles foaming up around the seasonal scent of cinnamon and orange, and go to my bedroom to rummage through my drawer of notebooks. I pull out the assortment of books: a kaleidoscope of beautiful bindings. You used to sit on my bed after your bath, your wet hair drying back into soft, dark springs, making a damp patch on your white nightdress. You would set out the notebooks in a circle around you before picking them up one by one. The soft aubergine suede one was your favourite; the one that I bought from a craft stall in Greenwich market during the year we lived with Timothy.

"What does it say?" You asked every time.

"All my secrets, Ceridwen."

"Can I read them when I've learnt to read squiggly writing?"

"No, you can't."

"I can read this. Look, this is my name."

At the bottom of the drawer is an unused book, the cover a thick slice of purplish-blue velvet; your Christmas present to me last year. I pull it out and reach into my bag for the silver pen covered in Celtic knot designs; the one Nain bought from the gift-shop at Conwy Castle on one of her educational expeditions to show you your heritage.

"You can read this one, Ceridwen," I tell the empty room.

In the bath I begin composing lines in my head, the way I compose poetry late at night when I should be falling asleep. In the living room, dried and dressed in the pink flannel pyjamas that you always laughed at, I settle onto the sofa: two slices of hot toast with real butter, a whole pot of fresh coffee, pen and notebook at my side. On the mantelpiece two sticks of vanilla incense burn: plunder from your room, their scent reminding me of the Victoria sponge cakes I baked for each of your birthdays.

December 18th 2003
Dear Ceridwen

It is almost six months now since you went missing. I'm waiting for you to come home, and, while I wait, I decided to write you a story.

We lived here at Tŷ Gurig until you were six months old. Timothy rang every day to try to persuade me to live with him in his cramped flat off the Bermondsey Rd and, in the end, we moved.

The smell was what shocked me most about London: the taste of pollution always on my tongue. The tap water was flat and dead after it had seeped through so many other bodies. It was no place for a baby, but Timothy was on course for a partnership and constantly told me we'd have a house in Greenwich or even Blackheath one day. It always seemed to me that the heath and Greenwich Park had more square feet of dog turds covering them than grass, but I didn't like to sully Timothy's dream.

When I met Timothy, on holiday in France, his tendency to be possessive seemed so romantic, but the shine wore off when he began cataloguing my every move, keeping mental lists of who I spoke to, whether I smiled when I spoke to them, whether I moved my head closer to listen when one of his friends was making conversation. I should have seen it coming, but instead I tried harder to placate him, tried to convince myself that his jealousy was something else; something tender and adoring. It was my dream, to be part of a family with a mother and a father. I wanted that for you, but not that much. He didn't have to hit me twice.

Back at Tŷ Gurig there was no lawyer's salary to live on, only Nain's pension and the odd boost of money when she sold a painting to a local gallery. It was good to be back in the fold of the mountains, the rain cocooning us from the world, Nain's lamb cawls to comfort us. But living off Nain and benefits didn't appeal, despite her protests.

The job in Bristol was ideal. Writer in residence with East Bristol Library Services sounded wonderfully glamorous and the humane hours were a bonus. So there we were, in a little rented Victorian house on Ruby Street, a stone's throw from Eastville Park, within cycling distance of the library, and round the corner from Trinity Street with its whole row of shops crammed with Asian and West Indian vegetables.

I think we would have met Caro and Stephen sooner rather than later. Everyone in the area seemed to know them. The Soulful Living Community occupied two big double fronted houses facing the park, both owned by a woman called Clare, though Stephen and Caro never seemed short of money themselves in those days.

You were almost three when we moved to Bristol. Bryn was home from the States.

"Are you going to be alright here, Bethan?" Bryn looked the spit of Dad in the photos, sleek mousy hair neatly brushed back, unlike my unkempt mane, and soft blue eyes like rain on slate, not like the brown eyes I'd inherited from Mam and Nain. Nain always said Welsh men were built like corgi dogs for the mines; long backs and short legs, compact and powerful, but Bryn was a copy of our English dad, long all over.

"I'm going to be fine. Thanks for all this Bryn. I don't know how I'd have managed without you."

"Ah, but you would manage though, wouldn't you? You're a Prichard woman."

I smiled and shrugged up at him. I was Bethan Loxley when we went to live with Nain, but I told her I wanted her name for my seventh birthday.

I met Caro later that day, in the doctor's surgery. She had one of those long double buggies with one baby behind the other. They were, about seven months old and pale skinned like their mam. Caro had the look of a Viking princess, I thought, and it was reassuring to be invited to someone's home in a strange, new neighbourhood.

Caro's front door was purple, side by side with a second purple door in the next house along; mirror images. The carefully painted signs above each door were almost identical too: *Soulful Living Community House 1, Soulful Living Community House 2.* Inside, the air was heavy with incense and the kitchen was full of the smell of spices. Three women sat around a big circular table. Caro was dressed in a white kaftan over pale blue silk trousers, her feet bare, tiny bells tinkling from the cord around her waistband. Her blond hair hung straight to her waist.

"I'm so glad you came, sweetie." She had a loud, confident voice and spoke as though we were old friends.

You squeezed my hand more tightly.

"Come and meet everyone." She waved a hand over the women assembled around an assortment of jewel coloured mugs filled with steaming fruit teas.

"This is Clare, our angelic benefactor." A woman in her thirties with limp mousy hair nodded in my direction. "And Juliet, who lives next door with her gorgeous girls."

Juliet smiled in my direction, a small, neat woman with strawberry blond hair in an expensive cut. I took in the three little girls who were concentrating hard on building a wooden block marble run on the kitchen floor.

"Say hello, cherubs," Caro said, in the children's direction.

"Hello," three voices chorused without looking up. They had their mother's pale, freckled skin and fine hair, slightly redder.

"Good girls. This is Heloise, she's our big girl, she's six, and Freya, whose just a bit older than Ceridwen, I think, and Caitlin."

Caro turned back to the table, to the last woman who was jiggling both of Caro's babies on her lap, "And this is Lynne, who is my absolute rock."

Lynne smiled, not taking her eyes off the babies, "Pleased to meet you," she said quietly. She was a small, square shaped woman with cropped brown hair and tiny eyes.

"And this, of course, is Bethan and her goddess of a daughter Ceridwen." Caro introduced us with a flourish of her arm.

"Hi." It sounded lame as soon as it came out.

"Stephen's upstairs working at the moment," Caro said in an almost reverential tone. "He's a writer like you. He can't wait to meet you, Bethan." She turned to you, "Would you like a rice cake, sweetie?"

"Yes, cake please," you said. You looked puzzled when she handed you the flat, dry rice cake.

13

"Look, Mam." You turned the crumbling circle of compacted rice grains around in your hands, as though it might turn into cake if you looked hard enough.

"It's a bit different from ordinary cake, cariad." I laughed nervously, "Have a bite." You nibbled your way through a tiny segment and wrinkled your nose.

"Yes, cake please," you repeated in case Caro had accidentally given you the wrong thing.

"We'll buy a cake later, love." I whispered, pulling you to me as I sat on the chair being offered by Juliet.

"You don't let her eat sugar do you, Bethan?" Caro asked, wide eyed, but smiling.

"Well, I…"

"I'll give you some leaflets, sweetie. You probably have no idea how much harm some foods can do to developing little bodies. It's a minefield trying to parent our children with all the pressures on us from the modern world. Stephen's writing a book about it." I could see Lynne nodding emphatically as Caro spoke. "Would you like a drink?"

I eyed the mugs on the table, "Well, if it's no trouble, coffee if you have it."

"I'm afraid we don't keep stimulants in the house."

"Right. Maybe a glass of water then."

"And Ceridwen?"

I hesitated, not wanting to make any more gaffs with the only people I knew in a strange city. I guessed that squash would be out of the question and wondered if there was anything wrong with juice, but you were ahead of me, "Blackcurrant, please."

"Of course, sweetie. We get this wonderful sugar-free, organic cordial from the whole food store on Trinity Street. Harvest. Have you found it?"

"I haven't found much yet, but the vegetable shops are good. I found this amazing cheese shop on a side road off Whiteladies Road when we went exploring Bristol a couple of days ago. I…" I was talking too fast.

"Cheese shop?"

"Yes, it's…"

"We don't eat dairy products."

I bit my lip. Five minutes and already I was offending them. I smiled uneasily, you saved the moment again as Caro handed you the blackcurrant juice.

"Diolch."

"Pardon, sweetie?"

"It's Welsh," I put in, "she's saying thank-you."

"Adorable!" Caro enthused, stroking your curls as she sat next to us.

Within a month I was talking Soulful Parenting with the best of them, inspired by Caro. At home I couldn't quite bring myself to stop baking cakes to Nain's recipes or refuse you the occasional bar of white chocolate, but I never mentioned these things to Caro.

Perhaps my inclination never to answer back was the root of all our troubles. On the day my parents left me and Bryn with Nain to go house hunting in Oxford I screamed and cried to go with them. My mam finally left in tears, looking back anxiously at me while Nain held me and tried to cajole me to wave good-bye. When they didn't come back I cried myself to sleep night after night, thinking that if only I hadn't fussed when they left somehow the car crash would never have happened. Some irrational part of me resolved never to upset anyone again.

In Caro's presence I was suddenly aware that I'd never given much thought to parenting. You were born at Tŷ

15

Gurig, which Caro heartily approved of, regretting that she'd lost the battle to have her twins at home, but proud that she hadn't given in to the suggestion of a caesarean section. After you were born, I simply fed you and did whatever you seemed to need.

Caro told me I was an instinctive Soulful Parent, "Perhaps it was growing up with an artist and wise woman or living close to the Earth in the mountains," she said. "You're so blessed to have this natural connection between your body and Ceridwen's. You wouldn't believe the harm my upbringing inflicted on me. I have to fight every inch of the way to find that space inside myself where I can give to my girls. That's why learning Soulful Parenting has been my salvation. All my instincts were so crushed, without the teaching I'd never be able to submit my will to the needs of their souls."

I was relieved to be told that I was instinctively soulful, but I still had a lot to learn. Each week, we sat in circle of brightly coloured velvet cushions on the floor of the big living room, the babies sucking wooden rattles and climbing around Lynne, who always sat slightly out of the circle to assist with Indigo and Xanthe.

"Lynne, sweetie, I think their nappies should be changed soon." Caro always smiled when she spoke. "And that gorgeous organic spinach needs just lightly steaming to puree down for their tea. You can bring them here to me while you're cooking."

Caro turned her smile on me, "That reminds me, Bethan. I know you love those cute little Asian veg shops, but you know they hardly carry any organic produce. I think you would be better off shopping at Harvest."

"I'm not sure I can afford…"

"Nonsense, sweetie. What we afford is all about priorities and what could be more important than putting the purest food into the temple of your child's soul? Isn't that right my little goddess?" She smiled over at you, playing with an assortment of little girls whose mothers were ranged around the circle.

"Isn't it odd how they're all girls?" I blurted out.

"What's that, sweetie?"

"I suppose I just noticed. All of us have daughters, but no sons."

Caro simply smiled at me, tilting her head to one side, as though she were about to explain how to boil an egg to someone who was a little slow.

"That's a very important point you've made, Bethan. You see the souls of boys and girls develop so differently, at least that's how it's meant to be if they are given the right space. The male and female essences are quite distinct. They each have their own purity and their own gifts. That's why the training for Soulful Parenting follows two beautiful, but distinct paths. I'm really only qualified to teach the goddess path, having girls myself. We think it's so important that the girls' souls are honoured and nurtured for their feminine uniqueness. That just can't happen if they are overshadowed by budding bringers at this early stage."

"Bringers?"

"Our soulful name for little boys."

A bit airy fairy, Nain would have said, but wholesome food, cloth nappies, cotton clothes, wooden toys, no sugar and no television didn't start any alarm bells ringing. I felt privileged to have found these wise people who took me under their wing.

*

I look up at the clock, it's after nine and I realise that I'm ravenous.

'You should put a nice cawl on, girl. You'll be skin and bone if you only live on toast, mark me.'

"Not tonight, Nain. It's too late to start defrosting chunks of lamb. Maybe tomorrow."

'You should take some out of the freezer tonight then. You have to look after yourself, you know."

"Okay, Nain. I'll do an omelette now and take some lamb out for tomorrow. Happy?"

There is no reply, only scratching on the living room door.

"Hey there Daisy, where've you been all day?" I scoop up Daisy's plump, purring body. "Come down with me and get some food." I set her down and she pads after me, winding round my legs.

"There you go, Dase." I say, pouring biscuits into her bowl. "You and me have to stick together."

I reach into the fridge for eggs. "One omelette coming up." I'm grateful for Daisy to talk to. "Then a bath and bed." Daisy glances up at me, yellow-green eyes like the shiny buttons on your favourite cardigan when you were five. "I know I've already had a bath today, but it's better than Prozac, Daisy – baths, poems and novels, the only way to sleep."

18

Caro I

Caroline Beaumont. Caro. I don't look my age in photographs, but some days I feel it. Almost fifty; some days I feel a hundred and then some. Who wouldn't after what I've been through? Some days it feels like everyone I've ever known has abandoned me.

Of course, I've got Justin. He's absolutely devoted to me and I'm grateful, naturally. When we made love last week he told me that I need to be taken care of, but he sees my inner strength too. It's so important to have someone who understands; a man who is willing to put my needs first. Not that everything is always sweetness and light with Justin. Sometimes even he forgets how vulnerable I am, but at least he's quick to realise when he's upset me, which is more than Stephen ever managed. Sometimes, though, I worry that Justin isn't everything I deserve.

We met when I was at one of my lowest points. I thought I'd go mad after I found out about Stephen cheating on me. Of course, even before that, Stephen was never there for me emotionally. As for sex - most of the time he simply wasn't interested.

"Schoolgirls?" I was appalled at the thought of that.

"It's just a game, Caro." He had a tone of voice that made me feel small, like I was a silly little girl with her first bout of PMT.

"I'm not dressing up as a schoolgirl for you," I spat back.

We were in our bedroom, the only room in the house that I ever thought of as my own. From where I was standing I could see the trees in Eastville Park. The leaves

19

had turned orange and yellow and were dropping onto the surface of the empty boating lake.

"You don't have to be submissive."

"What?" I felt as though I wanted to crawl out of my body. Across the park a lone jogger was circling the lake. I concentrated hard on his movement, trying to keep myself in place.

"You can fight back if you want. I like it."

"You're sick."

"Caro, it's a game."

"You'd better find your schoolgirl somewhere else. It's not going to be me." I quickly wiped a stray tear from the corner of one eye. I'd felt the same useless fury when I was a teenager, facing my holier-than-thou father, who knew all the right buttons to press.

I walked out of the room and downstairs. In the kitchen too many people were trying to cook dinner. I took refuge in the living room, lighting joss sticks to blot out the smell of cooking. Perhaps I was over-reacting. I wandered back to the kitchen and stirred vegetables in the wok.

"It's okay, Caro, everything's under control here," Lynne said, smiling, even though it was a bad idea with teeth like hers.

Stephen appeared at the kitchen door. "Dinner's nearly ready, sweetie." I said lightly.

He walked past me towards Lynne and the others assembled for dinner. "Smells delicious Lynne, I don't know what we'd do without you," he said.

To find out that he was sleeping with Lynne of all people. I know looks aren't everything, but everyone says I'm beautiful. I have blonde hair that doesn't come out of a bottle. My figure is good, statuesque even, and what did

Lynne have? A boiler suit, bad teeth, piggy eyes and a squat little body. I've always been taught to look for the beauty on the inside and I do, I really do, but something like that would shake anyone's generosity.

"You have to understand, Caro. Who I'm shagging has nothing to do with you or the girls. It's an irrelevance. Our marriage isn't about limiting who we are or who we relate to. It's about providing a place to grow in. It's about our shared commitment to giving a safe place to the girls. You know very well that it's from our togetherness that we can move out to fulfil other parts of ourselves, sexual or work related or whatever we need. But we always come back to this anchorage, you and me together for the girls, Caro."

We were in Bethan's living room when he made that particular speech. I'd crawled there the week before when I found out about his sordid affair with Lynne. Bethan sat on the futon next to me. I could tell she was reluctant to be there, but Stephen had pleaded with her to mediate. Stephen came over to the futon from Bethan's scruffy little red settee, some horse hair stuffed relic that she'd found in a junk shop in Clifton. I've no idea why Bethan bought that futon either, a monstrously uncomfortable contraption with a cheap cream cotton throw across it. Stephen knelt in front of me and held my hands while he went on talking. His piercing blue eyes locked onto mine. I felt that pull to surrender to whatever he said. And I was so tired. But I couldn't help feeling resentful.

"I'm not talking about the girls. I'm talking about you and me. What about fidelity?" I stopped so that he wouldn't hear the crack in my voice. "You never want to have sex with me, but you'll do it with… with that sad excuse for a woman!"

"Caro! That remark's beneath you. You know I love you, Caro, but Lynne is able to fulfil certain... certain needs, things that are not in your integrity. You've made it quite clear that there are things you won't do and I wouldn't ask you to go against your soul, Caro, but it's important that our needs are met so that we can be free to concentrate on our spiritual callings in this life. You shouldn't get hung up on these things, they're ephemeral. Lynne has needs too, Caro. It's an arrangement that works for everyone."

I felt Bethan move uncomfortably next to me. I wished she would leave. It wasn't as though she was mediating. She hardly spoke a word.

"But we're married." I buried my face in the throw, which I noticed had a coffee stain on it, and sobbed.

"Come on Caro," Stephen crouched over me, stroking my back, but there was no feeling in it, "Fidelity isn't about who's shagging who." I wheeled round to object to that horrible word, but he caught hold of my shoulders and locked my gaze. "Fidelity is our act of commitment to this central relationship. It's a spiritual bond that makes the world a safe place for our beautiful girls. The rest is just dispensing with the distractions. Anyway, with Lynne it was hardly about my needs at all. It was much more about her needs."

I thought of shouting at him that he'd just said Lynne fulfilled 'certain needs' in him, that he was already contradicting himself, but I was so tired. I wanted to be held and loved. Maybe he would be sorry, I thought. Maybe he'd start buying me presents and running bubble baths. I nodded childishly, ready to give in, but something in me rallied and I came to my senses, "Piss off, Stephen!"

Stephen skulked back over to the sofa and slumped down. We sat in tense silence for a while until he looked up, "I've sent Lynne away, Caro. I sent her away for you."

"What? Where's she gone?"

"Does is matter? I think she knows someone in Liverpool, but that's not the point. The point is, only you and the girls really matter, Caro. You are my soul keeper."

Bethan wriggled again, but I was too upset to take much notice of her. My marriage was on the line and I didn't want to end up alone like her.

"You sent Lynne away?"

"Of course, darling. Will you come back home with me? Now? I think we need some time."

I nodded again.

"Good girl. That's your gift, Caro. You are so beautiful when you are giving. You know it's what makes you grow as a spiritual being."

I nodded again.

I met Justin at a Soulful Parenting workshop. We shared all the same values.

"Caro. Short for Caroline Beaumont." I held my hand out for him to shake, sensing the way he was appraising me.

"Have you been to many of these?" he asked.

"Oh yes, I used to live with Ralph and Annabel in the very first Soulful Living House. I co-lead a Soulful Living Community in Bristol now, though I couldn't come to workshops much when my girls were small. Of course I read every new book Ralph writes and I've practiced Soulful Parenting since they were babies, but now that my girls have started to grow away from the Magical Bond

Phase, it's lovely to be able to come to these events. The pressures of the world are so against us."

"I know what you mean. I wish you could talk to my wife about it."

"She isn't here with you?" I scanned the crowd lining up for fair trade fruit teas or gathering in clumps of acquaintances from past workshops. I don't think I'd ever met a man alone at a Soulful Parenting gathering.

Justin smiled. He looked sad and wistful and very sexy. "Sadly, no."

"How old are your children?"

"Child. One boy. He's nearly three. Yours?"

"Twin girls. They're seven."

"And you live in a real Soulful Living Community? You must be quite the expert."

"Well, there's always more to learn. I'd love to go to some of the new *Attuning to the Universe* workshops that Ralph and Annabel run up in the Hebrides. I hear the place is so inspirational. My husband's been twice, but he doesn't think I should leave the girls for a whole week, not while they're still in the Intuitive Blossoming Phase. "

"And you think he's right?"

I laughed, nervous, a little embarrassed, but I didn't have to pretend to buy into any of that politically correct feminist stuff at a Soulful Parenting gathering. "I just think my nurturing role is very important to my girls and for my own spiritual development for that matter. I don't want to jeopardise it for any of us."

"Wow." He looked at me with such admiration.

I felt a melting sensation tingling down through my gut. He reminded me of Dave when I first met him, strong and sensitive.

"My wife's a lawyer," Justin went on. "She wanted to put Dominic into day care when he was six weeks old, but I just couldn't bear it. I'd been made redundant, but I had plenty of offers. I could have made good money, but it just seemed so cruel. I'm not saying I could replace the Magical-Mother Bond. I've had to come to terms with the fact that Dominic lost out on that and he'll need to work on those issues himself one day, but I've done what I could for him."

"Wow." I said in return. I wanted to let him know how much I sympathised. I wanted to do other things for him as well. I had needs too and Stephen had said we should deal with needs so that we wouldn't be distracted by them? "So what does your wife think about Soulful Parenting?"

"She calls it a load of touchy feely mumbo jumbo. It's like you said, the need for support gets even more urgent as children grow, especially if you're a lone voice. Most of Dominic's friends spend hours in front of the telly. I can just imagine them in the future: playing god-awful video games, shooting the life out of cartoon grannies for fun. They're all chockfull of sugar and E numbers, dumbed down so that all they want is to buy into the next craze."

How could I not fall in love?

It's so important to have Justin in my life. No-one else has ever made me his number one priority. And I'm so alone now. I suppose it's ironic that I've got Lynne around to help again, though she owes me a lot after what she did with Stephen. The children adore her, so I see her more to meet their needs than my own. But that's not much support in a whole world of hostility. Justin and Lynne, that's all I have. Everyone else has deserted me, Bethan,

Juliet, Dave… all of them. I'll be fifty in two months time.

All I can do is trust that the Universe has a lesson for me, but it hurts. Some days I cry and cry. It's hard on Indigo and Xanthe to see me so broken. It seems like every day now there is some new betrayal, another shock that I have to deal with. The only thing I can do is take charge of my reactions. That is my power. Whatever life sends my way I'm determined to transform it into something good, but it takes a lot of energy.

A few days ago I was out shopping with Indigo and we ran into Clare. She wouldn't even talk to us. I can't imagine cutting someone like that when they have a child with them.

"Clare, I'm really glad I ran into you. Do you think we could talk?" She was choosing a book in the shop at the top of Park Street, a novel, I think. She never read novels when she was in the community. Stephen disapproved of fiction, though he always made allowances for Bethan.

"Clare, do you think we could talk?"

All those years of living soulfully with her and she turned her back on me. She carried her stupid novel over to the guy at the counter and handed him a ten pound note as though I didn't exist.

"Clare?"

The guy behind the counter, a student-type with floppy hair, looked more embarrassed than she did. "Er, I think that lady's trying to talk to you," he mumbled, shifting from side to side a bit as he rang up her book and handed her change.

"That's not someone I want to talk to, thank you."

Can you believe that? And with Indigo there too. It beggars belief. Indigo stood there, watching it all, tears welling up in her eyes.

26

Of course the one that hurts most is Bethan. The girls were tiny when we met her and I was so vulnerable after having the twins, but I still gave her so much support. I'd gone to the doctor one day, even though Stephen didn't approve. I know he's right about not filling our children with poisons that destroy the Universe's laws, but Xanthe had been coughing for weeks and I ached for sleep. Stephen didn't sleep in the bedroom with us that first year so that the Magic-Mother Bond would be wholly honoured. I appreciated that it was a gift to us, but sometimes at night I couldn't see the logic of being alone with the girls. Anyway, in the end, even Stephen was glad I'd slunk off to the doctors because he was sure that Bethan and Ceridwen were meant to be a part of the community.

"Are they identical?" This woman asked in a voice with a slight accent. She had dark hair full of wild curls that fell just below her shoulder and eyes the colour of chocolate, the good quality organic sort that isn't full of milk and sugar.

"Yes. Indigo and Xanthe." I was proud of the girls' names. Stephen chose them for the colours of their auras at the moment the girls were born, dark blue and flaming yellow. "I'm Caro. Caroline Beaumont." I added.

The woman wore long beaded ear-rings, a dark red velvet skirt and boots with dark red and brown patches. The boots were leather, I noticed, thinking that Stephen wouldn't approve, but she looked good in them.

"I'm Bethan."

Welsh I thought, placing the accent.

"We've just moved in so I came down to register with the doctor."

"That's very organised."

"Not really. I've got my brother staying. He helped me move in and I've got a great list of things to do before he goes back. Making use of my captive babysitter."

"You've got children?"

"A little girl, Ceridwen. She's nearly three."

"Ceridwen? That's lovely. It's a goddess' name, isn't it?"

"Yes, goddess of poetry. I'm a writer see, and Nain approved of a Welsh name, so everybody wins." She laughed.

"What brought you to Bristol?"

"Ah, messy split and the need for a job, I'm afraid."

"I'm sorry. I didn't mean..."

"That's okay. He was a bit miserable, better off really."

Xanthe coughed in her sleep. Babies should be in arms, but Stephen let me use the bug for occasions when I had to leave the house alone with both of the girls, which wasn't often. I hoped they wouldn't come to too much emotional harm. "I'm afraid I need to get the girls home, but maybe you'd come and have a drink with us sometime."

"I'd love to. I hardly know a soul here yet," Bethan confided. I felt it must be a good sign that she called people 'souls'.

"Good. We're at 10 Park View."

"Ah, I know that one. Faces the park, right? I'm just around the corner in Ruby Street. When's a good time?"

"Oh, any afternoon, I'm always there." I almost danced home from the doctor's surgery. I wasn't even afraid to tell Stephen where I'd been. I knew I'd been sent to meet Bethan and that he would approve of her. The leather boots might be a problem and leaving a two year old little girl with her brother was on the questionable side, but we all have things to learn. We could help Bethan.

Bethan was a wonderful cook and she used to clean the place from top to bottom for me when Lynne was in one of her strops. Now Bethan hates me and tells lies about me, but it's all Chinese whispers, so I can't defend myself.

When I'm in my strong-soul place I know I've done nothing wrong. I know they are all afraid and I can even understand it. What happened was horrible, they're bound to look for someone to blame and it seems as though it's not enough for them to blame Stephen. But I have to stay strong. I have to refuse to take it all onboard. I have to be strong for Indigo and Xanthe, as well as for myself.

It makes me weep to think of the people who have walked out of our lives. Dave won't even look at me. After Bethan and Juliet began warning everyone about Stephen, Dave came round to my new house and screamed at me. He actually dared to accuse me of putting his daughter at risk, as though I would ever do anything to hurt Genevieve. All our years together, he had no problem going behind his wife's back or risking losing his daughter when he wanted me, and now he won't even listen to me. I know I've found a new strength in all of this, but I feel so fragile, so very alone. I don't know how I'd go on living if I didn't have the girls. The awful truth is that people have been abandoning me all my life. It was my mum first, when I was twelve.

"This isn't about you, darling. You know things have been strained between me and Daddy for a long time. Now that he's got his preferment he can't accuse me of ruining his career by leaving him."

She was packing the last of her things into a suitcase. She wasn't taking much. A couple of boxes were already in her car outside on the big circular driveway of the new house.

29

I stared out of my mother's bedroom window so that she wouldn't see the tears forming at the corners of my eyes. From here no one would guess that there were other big plush houses just a stones throw away, hidden beyond the trees. We'd only been here for three weeks, since my dad was made Archdeacon. Everything was timed so that the induction service, or installation, I forget all that jargon now, would fit in with the school holiday.

"You're not just leaving him, you're leaving me!" I was crying so hard that the words came out choked instead of the furious I was aiming for.

"You can contact me anytime, sweetie. You know I love you very much, but quite honestly... well after fifteen years with Daddy, I really need my space, Caroline."

"It's not your space, it's hers!" I was shouting now, into my enraged stride.

"Louise won't be there all the time, Caroline. It's her holiday cottage. She's coming to help me settle in and then she'll visit at weekends, but most of the time I'll be on my own. It's a chance for me to get my head round some things."

I choked back the next sob and balled my fists so hard that the nails bit into my palms. I liked the pain; it made me feel clear headed. I spoke more quietly, letting the words fall like fire crackers, "And at the weekend I suppose the thing you'll be getting your head round is Louise."

"Caroline! How dare you speak to me like that? You have no understanding of these things, and nor should you."

"I know what a lesbian is, Mum."

"Go to your room. I have no intention of talking to you while you're in this mood."

She left me with my dad. I used to wish they'd both abandoned me at birth. After mum left my dad was colder than ever, but I could cope with coldness. It was when he got that look in his eyes that he really frightened me. It didn't make me behave, though. Things simply escalated the older I got. I swear he got off on punishing my evil flesh, though he never ceased telling me it was for my own good.

"I'll tell your precious Bishop!" I screamed at him one day as he stalked from the room leaving me on the bed, the welts still vibrating with pain.

He stopped at my bedroom door. "There's no shame in disciplining a disobedient child, Caroline." He never raised his voice. He used the same stony-quiet tone whether he asked me to pass the salt at dinner or was telling me precisely the way in which he was going to beat me. His voice made me shiver whatever he was saying.

"You'll thank me one day for taking such an interest in your soul."

What did he know about having a soul?

I found solace in the arms, or rather other parts, of the boys like Danny Timms. Danny had no interest in my soul, but he shared my father's fascination with pain. Getting pregnant was too predictable, too pedestrian, but it happened anyway.

My dad didn't want to know me after the abortion, so I dropped out of sixth form and found myself another saviour. Andrew picked me up from home in his car, a triumph dolomite with five gears, and flicked his cigarette butt in my father's direction in answer to the holier-than-thou ranting. It was 1971. I was seventeen and convinced that there was love in the world. It was 1976 before I finally escaped from him.

Miserable childhoods are ten a penny. It's the happy ones that are abnormal, but that's what I wanted for my girls – an abnormally happy childhood.

Dear Ceridwen II

I wake at 6.30 in the morning. I've always hated mornings. 'Such a night owl,' Nain used to tease, but these days I wake up early. The daily realisation that you are not there is like tumbling out of warm blankets onto cold slate. I have a pattern for living here alone. First I make up the fire in the living room. I leave the air vents open while the coals catch and I go down to the kitchen. I light the stove there and make toast and coffee. By the time I've finished breakfast both fires are roaring.

If I hear Nain's voice badgering me to live on more than toast and eggs, I put a pot of cawl or vegetables for soup on the stove before I go upstairs. This morning she has no need to remind me. The lamb she insisted I defrost last night is in the fridge, ready for cooking. I cut the meat slowly, pulling apart the fat. While it browns, I chop vegetables and roll suet into dumplings, your favourite part. There is no word from Nain yet. I know where I get my night owl tendencies from.

In the living room I dampen down the vents on the larger stove and open room doors so that the heat will filter through the house. The heat edges along the corridor to Nain's studio, which is still lined with canvases, one or two forever incomplete, but it never reaches your bedroom; that door I keep tightly shut.

'There's a canvas I want to show you,' Nain says as I open the door to her studio.

"What?" I've stopped noticing that I talk out loud to my dead Nain.

'On the far wall, at the back of the stack. Go and have a look. I did it for you, girl.'

I carefully let each canvas fall onto my left arm. The last one is facing the wall and I struggle to lift it out and turn it. I sit down with it, tears falling silently. You look back at me, Ceridwen; my own dark curls, the eyes that I think of as Nain's, passed down to each girl in the family, your distinctive smile, always a little tongue in cheek, as though you concealed some permanent private joke.

"When did you…?"

'Last summer, cariad. Remember, she stayed a couple of weeks before you came. We were saving it for your fortieth birthday.'

"But my fortieth's not till next year, Nain."

'We were thinking ahead, love. She knows how to plan things, that girl of yours. And she knows how to look after things, including herself.'

"Did you know you were… that you were ill?"

'It might have crossed my mind, cariad. Can't go on forever you know, I had ninety-two years after all."

"Did Ceridwen know?"

'I think she saw how I was slowing down to a stop,' says and laughs softly, 'No-one could pull the wool over her eyes. But we didn't speak about anything. You should put that in your room, cariad. Keep her with you. She's not dead you know.'

December 19th 2003
Dear Ceridwen

Today I put up your picture in my bedroom, the portrait Nain did last summer. You are so beautiful. Nain says you are alive and I have to believe her.

You were a couple of months off your third birthday when we moved to Bristol. I had just over a month to find a nursery place for you so that I could begin my job in September. The first place we looked at was in Redfield, in an old church hall, only a twenty minute walk from home, well maybe thirty with a three year old. The nursery leader was a formidable looking woman in her fifties, tall and broad with grey hair that had a slightly purple tinge.

"We have a very structured day for them," she told me, "To get them ready for school. They have a drink at eleven and lunch at half past twelve. In the afternoon they are allowed to play on the outdoor toys if they have been well behaved in the morning."

"Well behaved?"

"Some of them forget to share, or whine to go home. No naughtiness and no crying is what we aim for. They soon get the hang of it. We have two story times, one after lunch before outdoor play and one at half five for those staying till the end of the day. I think you said you'd pick up... er, your little girl..."

"Ceridwen," I prompted.

In the corner of the room a nursery assistant was standing over a crying toddler, berating him.

"Quite, you said you'd be picking Ceri up at four, yes?"

"Ceridwen."

"We like to use short names to call them by to get their attention quickly. Would you excuse me a moment?"

She stalked towards the assistant and sobbing little boy and bent down. She took him by the arm and began to speak into his ear. I watched his eyes grow big, the way he sucked in his sobs and wiped his sleeve across his eyes. He nodded rapidly. She marched back to us, smiling broadly, and put a hand on your head, "It's so important that we help them learn self-control. If we train them at this age it saves years of heart-break later."

"Thank you, I think we should be going now."

"Pardon?"

"I don't think it's quite what we are looking for, me and Ceridwen." I emphasised your name like a defiant school girl, grabbed your hand and headed for the door. I had to pause to collect myself once we were outside in the bright August sunshine.

"Mam?" You looked full of concern and I realised I was shaking.

"I'm fine, cariad." I took a deep breath.

The next two places weren't much better.

"I feel so guilty, Nain," I told her on the phone, "I've never left her before, except the odd hour with you. The children in these places look so lost, so abandoned, like they've given up hope. I won't be able to do any work for worrying if I leave her somewhere like that."

"Something will turn up, Bethan, love, you see if it doesn't," Nain reassured. I was grateful she didn't tell me to give up and go back to Tŷ Gurig.

"I hope so, Nain. I've only got a couple of weeks left till my job starts."

I didn't tell Nain that at night I dreamt of my mam crying as she left me in Nain's arms the day my parents drove away. Instead I steeled myself, told myself I was twenty-six and it was time that I stood on my own feet.

"What are you doing for Ceridwen's birthday, love?"

"I haven't really thought yet. I've got a bit longer for that. We've met a couple of families that live in a community, so I could invite their children round for tea and do some games. I've just got to be careful what I feed them."

"Why's that then?"

"They're vegetarian, Nain, well, vegan actually."

"Bit joyless that, isn't it?"

"I suppose, but they put a lot of thought into it. They don't have sugar either."

"Not a lot left really. When you get to my age and you've been on your own as long as I have, chocolate's better than sex. I don't think I could give it up, chocolate that is."

I laughed. "Nain! Anyway, if you were vegan you could have dark chocolate."

"Ah well, I like a bit of variety, I do." She chuckled. I could imagine her curled in the big armchair by the picture window, her grey curls cut short, but still unruly, her plum coloured painting smock with the emerald pockets spattered with paint and a huge assortment of books piled on the big beech coffee table at her side.

"It would be lovely if you could come here for Ceridwen's birthday, Nain. I'd like you to see the place."

"Ah, well, I'm not one for travelling, never have been really, and I think I'm past getting on all those trains."

I didn't argue. I couldn't imagine myself wanting to do a six hour jaunt on three different trains at the age of eighty.

"We'll come to Tŷ Gurig for Christmas, then."

"Good girl. I'll make sure Mr. Evans Tal y Bont gets us a tidy tree and I'll order a turkey from Geraint. You get settled in nice now and don't worry about this nursery. It'll all work out, girl."

"Bethan, sweetie, you're looking so tired."

Caro ushered me into the living room. "Ceridwen, sweetie, would you like to play with the girls?" She looked across to me, "Juliet's darlings are out in the garden with her. Lynne's got my angels out there too. Then there's

Alicia and Genevieve. Why don't you go and see, Ceridwen?" Caro turned to me, "Alicia is Matt's daughter, an old friend of Stephen's from school days, and Genevieve's Mum lives a few streets away."

"Do you want to go in the garden, Ceridwen?" I asked.

"Show me." You put out a plump hand and I got up from the gold floor cushion to join you.

"That's alright, sweetie. I'll show you where the children are," Caro offered.

"Mam show me."

"It's fine," I told Caro, taking your hand and leading you through the passageway and kitchen to where the sound of little girls' voices made you forget your anxiety. You ran off without a second glance.

"You're very brave starting work, Bethan. I don't think I could leave the twins for an hour, even at that age."

I felt mean-spirited for even thinking that Lynne seemed to have the twins whenever I visited. At least Caro was at home with her children and still feeding the babies herself.

"I don't think it's what you'd call bravery, Caro. I have to work and this job is pretty humane really. The only problem is I can't actually find any childcare, well nothing that I'd be happy with. I've started looking for registered childminders, but they all seem to be full."

Caro ushered me back into the living room. It was quiet and cool in there despite the hot August day and smelled of jasmine incense.

"You can't possibly leave our little goddess with a stranger, Bethan. I wouldn't hear of such a thing. Stephen would never forgive me. She'll come here of course."

"But, I can't. I mean I wasn't hinting, I don't mean to impose."

"Nonsense. We'd be offended if you didn't let us look after her."

"It's very kind, but don't you have to be registered?"

Caro laughed and touched my arm from her perch on the purple cushion.

"Really, Bethan, you're so conformist. We have to strike out and live free lives in tune with the Universe and our true souls."

"I suppose, It's just that… well, I suppose they have these regulations for the children."

"Well, if you're leaving your child with a complete stranger it might be different, but we're friends, Bethan, more like family, really."

"You're very kind. I just…"

"Not at all. We adore Ceridwen. I couldn't sleep thinking of her in some nursery or with one those child minders you see dragging kids around shops, screaming at them constantly. So that's settled then."

So it was. And with you spending five days a week there, it seemed churlish to refuse to take up Caro's offer of Soulful Parenting classes. You seemed so happy ay the community house. They had to be doing something right.

I felt nervous at the first session, the one when I asked why there were no little boys in the community. I sat in the circle anxiously wondering if everything I'd done to bring you up so far would be held up to the spot light and found wanting, but they were kind and patient. I was relieved that there were some faces that I knew around the circle: Juliet and a woman I knew as Genevieve's mother, Annette. Caro introduced me to other women, her long arms making flourishing gestures as she spoke, her long pale hair clipped back with glittering star combs.

"This is Sophie. She has two little girls, Olivia and Hannah, and lives on your street, Bethan. And this is Rachel, who lives next door with Juliet and has a daughter, Lucy, who's just had her fourth birthday, and Paula, whose little girl, Katie, is just eighteen months. Paula's expecting another blessed event next March."

Everyone cooed and congratulated Paula.

At the next session I had another question. "No dads?"

"Well, that's another very important point." Caro smiled broadly and pressed her palms together. All eyes were fixed on her.

"There are several reasons why this absolutely must be a group for mothers. Soulful Parenting is for everyone, fathers and mothers, our growing goddesses and budding bringers, but as I told you before, when we are learning to parent soulfully we must never confuse the paths. As parents we not only bring up goddesses and bringers on their own pathways, it's also important that we recognise that adults contribute something unique to the formation of their little goddesses and bringers. It would be quite inappropriate for me to presume I could teach a father. My role is to teach those on my own pathway. Stephen has offered Soulful Parenting courses for the dads, but sadly, it is in the nature of bringers to be resistant to support."

I saw Sophie, Annette and Paula nodding emphatically. I could imagine the choice language that Timothy would have used in response to such an invitation.

"But what about single mothers? Are you saying our children can't grow up properly without both parents?"

I saw Juliet and Rachel lean forward for Caro's answer.

"If you isolate yourself it could be a disaster, Bethan, I won't lie to you. But that's the gift of our little community. By living here, or close to us, our goddesses have access to the adult bringers in the group. That's particularly Stephen's role, of course. I just know that Ceridwen will blossom under his influence."

"But isn't Stephen always in his study working?"

"Tiny goddesses need only a little interaction with grown bringers, Bethan. We don't want their souls overshadowed. Knowing he is there providing security and a centre to the home is most of what a little girl needs from her daddy figure at this age."

It sounded a bit like old fashioned sexism in new clothes, but it relieved me of feeling guilty about not having Timothy or some other man around to give you a proper, balanced childhood.

Caro told us repeatedly that living soulfully with our children was not a list of rules; we had to be true to the unique soul of each child. For all that, I soon had a list of what was approved and not approved.

"But it doesn't add up, Caro. I don't know how I can never thwart what Ceridwen wants, but still stop her from having all things that are frowned on – sugar and food with additives and all the rest. Not to mention television and plastic toys."

Caro was always patient. "If we fulfil our role as soulful parents properly there will simply be no contradiction between what our children desire and what it is best to give them," she explained.

We were in her living room, our second home. The bells on Caro's silk trousers tinkled as she leant forward on her purple floor cushion. She pressed her palms together, then let them fall to her side, her silver and moonstone bracelet emerging from her pale silk tunic.

"Why would truly soulful children, raised by soulful parents ever dream of wanting some cheap plastic doll when they can make peg dolls or have a lovely home made rag doll?" Caro asked. Heads nodded around the candlelit room. "It stands to reason that they won't want to eat sticky sweets or gulp down milk stolen from baby calves when they are brought up with their soulfulness intact."

I was the only parent in the group who continued to serve cakes made with butter. Sometimes I even cooked a chicken or a pot of lamb cawl on a winter day when I was missing Nain. I did it in secret. I was the only mother who bought poly-cotton pyjamas from the market rather than the expensive all cotton sets from the quaint little shops in Clifton that Caro recommended, although I had a cotton pair that I kept for the nights that you slept over at the community house. I still shopped at the Asian veg stores where bargains were always to be had, rather than buying organic produce from Harvest. My small acts of defiance put me into a state of perpetual self-questioning, but I reassured myself that guilt is the normal condition of all mothers.

"There's so much stress laid on the cognitive and cerebral these days," Caro told us. She looked stunning in a pale lilac kaftan that fell, in several diaphanous layers, over narrow white silk trousers. "I'm afraid we have only ourselves to blame. In trying to gain equality, the early feminists simply bought into the notion of becoming like men and sacrificing our essential goddess-nature. Rationality isn't all it's cracked up to be, you only have to look at the news to see that, which of course I know you always protect your little goddesses from." She shot me a questioning look, but smiled before going on, "Our feelings are our gift and we must never be afraid of our little ones' strong emotions."

Caro took a breath and sipped a glass of elderflower cordial, the recycled blue glass with its thin gold rim catching the light.

"Goddesses are the keepers of emotion and the balancing force to complement too much rationality in the world. It shouldn't surprise us that our little goddesses feel things very strongly. This is their gift. So often I see women out with their children, trying to stop their angels from crying or shouting. It is so damaging to their souls. You need to encourage them to give full rein to everything they feel. Help them to get it all out. Let them know that you hear what they are saying, whether it is rage or sadness or amusement, anything at all."

"But sometimes…"

Caro held up a warning hand, still smiling. "Bethan, we mustn't let embarrassment get in the way of saving our children's souls. Society is so repressed, but we shouldn't give in. If a little goddess wants to howl with grief in the street we must be in the moment, stare down ignorant passers by and let our angel give full vent. If she wants to dance down the aisles of a shop, then so be it."

I hunched down on my floor cushion feeling uneasy about my willingness to conform to the world outside. Was I emotionally repressive? Should I be encouraging you to cry and rage, even in public? The questions plagued me much more than my multiple sins of allowing you occasional chocolate bars or TV cartoons. I agonised even though you were such a sunny child. I was grateful when other mothers confessed their own struggles. Paula, whose second baby turned out to be a son, a chubby, happy little boy called Robert, had a husband who openly disliked Caro and more openly loathed Stephen. Her life was constantly pulled in two directions. My main ally, though, was Juliet. She and her daughters lived in the community, occupying the next door house to Stephen and Caro, along with the much more biddable Rachel and her daughter Lucy. Juliet had a way of persisting with her own life without openly asking questions. We giggled together about our disobedience and consoled each other about our failings as soulful parents.

"Hi Bethan." Juliet breezed in without knocking. She always looked elegant and poised, her strawberry blond hair trimmed to perfection, "Patel's have mushrooms cheap today. You should go round before they close."

"Thanks. Although I should say shame on you, buying non-organic mushrooms for your goddesses."

"I'm just all kinds of bad." Juliet laughed. "But if you don't tell on me, I won't tell that you forced me to drink your wicked coffee."

"Hint taken." I filled the kettle.

"You've got this place pretty nice, now, Bethan."

Juliet wandered round my kitchen-diner, a knocked through room at the back of my rented Victorian terraced house, which I gradually filled with the best junk shop furniture I could find, amassing kitchen implements along the way to rival Nain's back at Tŷ Gurig.

"Thanks. It's okay, but I'd like to buy a place really. Now that I've got this new post at the refugee project and some creative writing students on the side, I keep thinking I should put my money into something more secure."

"You're joking?" Juliet whirled round, her face a picture of mock horror so that her pink colouring rose.

"Not really. Why?"

Juliet sagged melodramatically into the armchair by the gas fire, "You mean you haven't had Stephen's lecture on the evils of ownership?"

"No. What's wrong with having a house? Clare owns the community houses and Stephen doesn't have a problem with that."

"Ah, that's different, my dear. You should be using your resources for the good of Soulful Living now, not selfishly investing in your individual future out of some sense of non-soulful mistrust in the Universe."

I bit my lip, unsure of how serious Juliet was being. "Do you think the Universe will just support me without me making any effort?" I poured hot water onto the coffee grounds and Juliet wrinkled her freckled nose appreciatively.

"My dear, the Universe always supports those who put their trust in it. If you insist on running yourself into the ground working for a living then you have only yourself to blame when the Universe turns on you."

I poured the coffee into two brightly coloured mugs, acquired from a gallery in Machynlleth the last time I'd visited Nain. "But do you believe that? I suppose it's what Caro and Stephen do. I have wondered how hardly anyone seems to work for a living in the community, if that's not an offensive thing to say."

"Not at all. I only manage because Clare rents the place so cheaply to us. It's her contribution to the community. Between that and what the child support agency extorts from my filthy rich ex husband, I can get by. Rachel is as poor as a church mouse."

"What about Stephen and Caro? I know Stephen beavers away in his study writing, but does he actually produce anything?"

"My dear innocent Bethan," she said in mock horror, "it's not about production. It's about the process." Juliet paused to sip coffee.

"But how do they live? They seem to have money."

"Stephen's dad is loaded. He has a mass of shares and properties he rents out in London. One day it will all be Stephen's. He's an only child. In the meantime daddy gives him whatever he wants as far as I can make out."

"But you said he disapproved of owning houses, except…"

Juliet giggled and peered over her coffee mug at me.

"The way Stephen sees it is that these things will be left to him for a purpose. It is the Universe's way of affirming the life that he and Caro have chosen."

"Do you really believe all this, Juliet?"

Juliet put down her coffee mug on the little pine table that I'd rescued from a skip and sanded and waxed myself. "I believe in not filling my children's bodies with poisons, though I'm not as puritanical as Caro would like. I believe in giving my girls a good start in life by being there for them and not filling their heads with a lot of mainstream crap and TV. Stephen and Caro can come across as zealots, but their hearts are in the right place. The way I look at it is that they make space for me to do things a bit differently. My parents fret about me and my ex thinks I'm bonkers, even though he lived here himself once upon a time, but I feel comfortable in the community. My only worry is that I can never be as good a mother or kind a person as Caro."

"You're a great mother, Juliet, and Caro does get a lot of help."

"I suppose she does, but she gives a lot too. Anyway I should get back. Rachel's watching the girls while I shop. I just thought you'd like to know about the mushrooms."

"Absolutely." I walked with Juliet down my hallway decorated with endless photographs of you between two of Nain's smaller canvasses, "Thanks, Juliet. Bye."

When you were coming up to five we had to think about school, but there was never much of a decision. Heloise, Freya and Lucy were already attending the small school in Montpelier and you would start at the same time as Olivia and Genevieve, followed the next year by Caitlin, Hannah and Katie and later by Indigo and Xanthe. The small school relied gratefully on the community for a steady flow of children, something that Caro emphasised to the rather nervous head-teacher whenever a part of their curriculum threatened to be out of step with the needs of our children's souls. I was impressed by the way she handled authority figures and grateful not to have to do myself. You loved the first class, where you stayed until just before your seventh birthday.

We had good friends, an income and a school you were eager to go to. Those were the golden days, Ceridwen.

Caro II

I can't believe what I've been through since January and all for nothing. Surely they can't think I'd have anything to do with those horrible things. I couldn't believe it when I heard that Bethan had waltzed off to Social Services and told them all sorts of lies. Then Juliet and the others jumped on the bandwagon. Of course, I tried to warn them for ages about Stephen, about how dangerous and manipulative he could be, but they ignored everything I said. Not that I had any idea of what he was up to. What none of them understand is that I'm more his victim than anyone. I always have been, though I didn't realise it myself for years. I was broken when he found me. I thought he was my saviour. I've done nothing but cry for the last three months. I'm amazed I have any tears left.

It was shortly after New Year when Bethan phoned. I'd been in my new house for a week and it seemed like everything in the place was conspiring against me. The plumbing in the tatty 1970s melamine kitchen leaked so that I had to have a bucket in the cupboard under the sink. If I slept in late it overflowed. The water pressure had something wrong with it so that the shower sputtered or ran suddenly cold, then scalding. The electricity meter ate cards in a blink, so I spent half my life queuing for top ups. And the place was filthy. I needed was cheering up.

"Caro, it's Bethan."

"Happy New Year, Bethan." The phone was in the hallway, the only place with a socket, so I had to stand in the dim draughty passage to talk. I flicked back my hair, recently trimmed with the roots touched up to keep my natural blond, and leant against the horrid paisley pattern wallpaper.

"What? Oh yes, it's New Year, I forgot. I'm afraid it may not be a happy one. Have you spoken to Stephen since you got back?"

"Only briefly when I picked up the twins. He did say you'd had a misunderstanding, but I didn't hang around."

"A misunderstanding?"

"Yes."

"Right. Look Caro, it's a lot more than a misunderstanding." There was an uneasy pause. When she started to talk again, her voice cracked, which wasn't like Bethan. She's always been too held together for her own good. I don't think I'd ever even seen her cry in all the years I'd known her.

"Caro, Stephen has been… I mean Ceridwen told me that Stephen… He's been…" I heard her take a deep breath, "abusing her."

"What?" I felt as though the vile paisley spirals would suck me in. I started to cry. Bastard! Even now that I'd left him he was going to go on ruining my life.

"I don't know whether it's just Ceridwen, Caro. I mean there are so many girls there all the time, the twins and Juliet's girls and …"

"No, there can't be anyone else, Bethan." I leant more heavily against the wall; the paper had a musty smell of old sweat and cabbages. It made me want to retch.

"What do you mean, there can't be anyone else?" Bethan sounded brittle.

"I'm sure nothing has happened to Indigo and Xanthe. I'd know about it if it had. I'm sure I would." It was hard to talk through my tears.

"How would you know?"

"I'm just do. Stephen's a bastard, but I know him well enough to know he'd never touch Indigo or Xanthe."

"Well, even if you're right, what about the others?"

"They're not like that, Bethan."

"What?"

She was angry now, but still cold. I wished instantly that I hadn't said that. I should have known Bethan would take it the wrong way.

"I only meant, well, Juliet's girls are pretty feisty, Bethan, they'd be too... I mean... I'm really sure that he couldn't get away with anything with them. I've known them since they were babies."

"I'm not sure what you're saying." Bethan could sound very brusque at times. I put it down to growing up in that cut off little place and being brought up by an old woman. I always made allowances.

"I think maybe Stephen had an obsession with Ceridwen," I said, trying to sound soothing, "I mean, I suppose he must have. I'm sure that's it, Bethan. In fact, now I come to think of it, he's always talked about Ceridwen in a different way. After that dreadful holiday we had together Stephen was beside himself, worrying that you might keep Ceridwen away from the community. He hardly ate for a week."

"And you didn't think I'd be interested in that?"

"Oh you know what he's like. I thought it was just Stephen being melodramatic about losing an acolyte. He's always had that guru thing going on. In any case, you came to your senses and it all blew over, so there wasn't any need to dwell on it."

Bethan spoke quietly, but I could feel the chill down the phone line, "It's the sort of thing that would worry me, if a man I lived with couldn't eat because he might not see someone else's child, I'd be pretty alarmed."

"I don't think you can know that, Bethan. Anyway, it wasn't like that exactly, I'm probably not telling it right and I had so much on my mind. You know how difficult my life has been. What did Ceridwen say Stephen did to her exactly?"

"I don't want to talk about it on the phone."

"Yes, well, it must be hard, but I think I need to know, sweetie. I mean how am I going to handle this with Indigo and Xanthe? I can't risk having them upset by this."

"I've got to go now, Caro."

"Bethan, wait, I need to know what… Perhaps I should come round?"

"Sorry, Caro, I can't… Not now. Ceridwen won't be seeing Stephen again, ever."

A sudden fear knotted my stomach. "But you won't go to the police?"

"I don't know. I'll speak to you again soon."

She put the phone down, leaving me reeling and with less than half the information I needed. I was frantic about what I could say if my girls asked something. I wiped my tears and went to the squalid little kitchen that overlooked a seedy concrete yard. I made a drink, chamomile tea with ginger to soothe. I was thankful that I'd dropped the girls off at Juliet's earlier, so that they hadn't had to overhear any of that. But then it hit me that I was alone. My world was crumbling around me and I didn't even have my gorgeous girls to hold onto. I sat on the cold, cracked vinyl floor in the unheated kitchen and howled.

*

51

I was back in the hostel at St. Jude's: a bone-thin twenty three year old with hair like dead straw. I can't remember how I found the place. Someone from the hostel had picked me up from hospital when I was discharged, my ribs still broken so that every breath was excruciating. The bruises on my face were turning a nauseating yellow-green. The volunteers were kind, but the counsellor didn't understand how much I'd been through. It wasn't only Andrew that I'd escaped from. Before him there was Danny and the abortion and my unholy reverend father with his belts and straps and willow thin canes that sang through the air before cutting welts into my skin. The counsellor droned on in his whiny-gnat voice about moving on, not being a victim and taking control. All I wanted was to be loved, but he wasn't interested; just whined on about professional boundaries.

I met Stephen after one of the counselling sessions. I'd run out in tears, humiliated by another rejection from the man who was supposed to be helping me. I huddled in the bathroom crying and Stephen came in. His dad was one of the benefactors of the hostel. Stephen used to volunteer for odd jobs, driving people to hospital, being around to listen to the horror stories.

He didn't say anything. He crouched next to me. He held me and rocked with me. When my sobs subsided he began to stroke my hair, teasing knots through the brittle ends, the way my mother used to before she left to live with Louise. He pulled out a clean handkerchief and patted my face dry, as though I was delicate, and then he kissed each of my damp eyes. His own eyes were so blue, so intense. I was mesmerised.

He helped me to my feet without a word and guided me to my narrow plain room with its white walls and ugly beige duvet. He began to undress me, slowly, silently. He was so gentle, like a father undressing a small child at bath time, though I couldn't remember anything like that from my father. He wrapped me in the duvet and lay down next to me, stroking my hair, never taking his eyes off me. I fell asleep imagining his eyes were soothing candle flames. It wasn't until I woke that he made love to me, not like Danny or Andrew made love, hard and greedy, but as though he saw me, as though I was a china doll.

Bethan agreed to come round and talk a few days after the New Year phone call. She looked pale and shaken, not at all herself, even her curls seemed lifeless. At least she was sweet about what I must have been through for all those years with Stephen. It was a relief for someone to realise how hard it had been for me with that manipulative, cruel bastard. I thought the conversation was going well, but then I apparently said the wrong thing.

"Bethan, you won't let me down for the party will you?" We were sitting in the living room of my new house. Lynne had painted it a warm ochre colour as a moving in present and I'd bagged some of the floor cushions and curtains from the old house, so it was a relatively civilised spot in an otherwise depressing place. I'd even been out and bought coffee especially for Bethan, real coffee.

"The party?" She looked at me as though I had grown an extra head.

"Indigo and Xanthe are thirteen next week, Bethan. It's so important, becoming a teenager. It's a huge thing, a rite of passage. They need all their friends around them. They're already upset that Heloise has to go back for the start of term. It's important that everyone is there for them,

53

especially Ceridwen. It wouldn't be the same without Ceridwen. The girls would be devastated."

"Are you having the party at Stephen's?" Bethan put her coffee mug down on the floor beside the red floor cushion and glared at me.

"I've got to, sweetie. This place isn't big enough and anyway it's still such a mess. I've hardly got any furniture yet. And he is their father, Bethan. The twins want to have their party at Stephen's and you'd be the last person to tell me that I should refuse them that on their birthday, surely. It's not like Ceridwen will be alone with him…"

"Have you any idea how much she's been through just to tell me about this, let alone what he's done? We're not going anywhere near the place, either of us."

She virtually spat the last words out. She looked rigid with tension, but I couldn't let my daughters down. I had to try to get through to her for their sakes.

"Maybe you should try to talk it through with Stephen? I could mediate for you, sweetie, the way you did for me and him when Lynne…" I trailed away, but managed to add, "I'm sure we can sort it all out."

"Sort it out?" She stood up so fast I flinched away from her. "You mean I should let myself be talked into understanding how this is all some freaky part of bloody Soulful Parenting that I haven't properly grasped? Maybe you can spin abuse into some kind of spiritual formative experience, but it won't work on me!" She began to pace the room, but she didn't cry. I wondered if Bethan had any tears in her.

"I didn't say anything of the sort. It's me you're talking to, not Stephen! You need to remember that no-one is as much his victim as I am. He's emotionally abused me for years and we never even had a sex life, not since... well I can hardly remember when."

I could feel the hot tears coursing down my dry skin. I should have stopped, but I was so hurt. I had to try to make her understand. "He wanted me to pretend to be a school girl for him and when I told him to look for it elsewhere he just turned off me completely. You have no idea how much my self esteem was destroyed by him. Most nights he didn't even sleep in my bed."

Bethan stopped pacing and swung round to face me. "What the hell are you saying, Caro?" Her face was red, puffy and ugly, but still not a single tear. "Can you hear yourself? You mean to tell me that you not only saw him crying over Ceridwen and said nothing to me, but you also knew he was into school girls and wasn't in your bed at night. Where the hell was he at night, Caro? Where the hell was he all the time Juliet and Rachel's kids lived next door with shared keys to both houses or when Ceridwen or any one of a dozen other girls were sleeping over?"

"He listened to the radio in his writing room. He liked to hear the news when the girls were asleep so that we could protect them from world events. You know their souls are too delicate to be subjected to all that violence and insanity..."

"I can't believe this!" She stormed towards the living room door and pulled hard on the handle, one of those cheap chrome handles from some mass DIY store.

"Bethan, don't go. We need to talk. Stephen sure you've simply misunderstood."

"Misunderstood?" she rounded on me from the door, "If you believe that you're a fool."

"Tell me what Ceridwen said then. I can't be expected to judge the situation or help my girls if you won't tell me what he's supposed to have done exactly."

"We don't need you judging the situation, Caro. I believe my daughter and what happened to her is private."

She turned and walked out, slamming the living room door and then the front door behind her. Alone, I dissolved in tears on the purple floor cushion. I might have sat and cried for hours if my precious girls hadn't heard the doors slamming and rushed down to me.

"Mum, Mum are you alright?" Indigo hesitated in the doorway, her long pale hair framing her slender face, her eyes a picture of concern.

Xanthe rushed straight in, threw herself on me and hugged me tight. We cried together and I motioned to Indigo to join us. We sat on the floor, cradling each other; my tears mixing with Xanthe's. Indigo stroked our hair, mine long and straight like her own and still as blond, Xanthe's soft and spiky, the tips coloured cerise.

"You shouldn't have talked to her, Mum," Xanthe told me.

"I had to try, my angel. I thought I could make sure she would let Ceridwen come to your party."

"Will she?" Indigo asked. It broke my heart to see how sad she looked.

"I don't think so, sweetie."

"Bitch!" Xanthe stormed, breaking into fresh tears.

"It's alright for you to cry too, Indigo." I told her gently. "You don't have to be strong for me. It's good to let your emotions out. They block the soul otherwise."

She nodded, but she didn't cry; only looked tired and disheartened.

Of course, Bethan didn't let Ceridwen come to the party and it broke the girls' hearts, but that wasn't enough devastation for Bethan. The morning after Xanthe and Indigo's birthday the phone rang. I stumbled downstairs to the gloomy hallway, cursing that I'd overslept and would have to deal with water from the overflowing kitchen bucket.

"Caro?"

"Hi, Bethan. Listen, sweetie, can I call you back? It's just that the leak in…"

"No, just listen."

"Pardon?" I could tell from her voice that she was about to drop another bomb.

"You left your girls with Stephen after the party?" She sounded so steely.

"Yes, but…"

"And Juliet's girls stayed over too?"

"Oh, but Bethan…"

"And who else?"

"Just the usual crowd, Bethan."

"You promised. You said no children…"

"Oh, but Bethan, it was their party and Lynne promised to watch Stephen and anyway he's told me nothing could happen, nothing even the least bit ambiguous. He's much clearer about the boundaries now and…"

"Juliet's here with me."

"What?"

"Heloise phoned from uni last night. She's split up with her boyfriend and was a bit drunk. When Juliet said that Freya and Caitlin were at Stephen's, Heloise told Juliet to go and get them out of there. Freya and Caitlin have told Juliet the same as Ceridwen told me. We're going to the police, right now. God, Caro, you promised me no children would ever be left in his care again."

"Bethan, it wasn't like that! Lynne was…"

"Shut up, Caro, I'm not interested. You'd better get your girls out of there, now."

"Bethan, wait!" I was crying now, trying not to let it show in my voice.

"If you want to come with us you can bring the girls here. They'll be fine together while we speak to the police. We'll have to tell them the names of the other children who stayed there."

I could feel myself shaking. The sobs choked out of me so that I couldn't speak.

"Are you coming with us, Caro?"

"I… I can't…" I managed and the phone went dead.

I still can't believe they did it. They actually went off to the police and said all kinds of terrible things to some police woman, who I heard Bethan got on with really well, probably because the policewoman was Welsh and took Bethan's side. They brought in some social worker too. I met her a few days later, a dumpy woman called Pam, with a permanently anxious expression, mousy hair and narrow little eyes. Bethan and Juliet told a pack of lies. In my more generous moments I remind myself that they didn't understand how complicated the truth was. I suppose they were right about Stephen in a way. He was a bastard, but they didn't notice when he was making my life hell.

I confronted Stephen as soon as Bethan rang off. With Bethan about to go to the police, I insisted he had to talk to me, but he refused to see me without Lynne there. He said it was best if someone impartial was there to mediate. As though Lynne could ever be impartial. She was more besotted with Stephen than ever since she'd returned. He ordered her around like a slave and she jumped to it, her puppy dog eyes brimming with gratitude. It was sickening. Anyone could see he was never going to sleep with her again, anyone but Lynne that is.

"Stephen, what the hell has Ceridwen said to Bethan?"

"You know what she's said." He leaned back in his plush reclining arm chair, a gift from Clare years ago, and sipped fruit tea.

"I don't know. Tell me!"

"You shouldn't get upset, Caro. I remember a time when you were so earthed and centred. I know the real Caro is still in there." He smiled at me, thin lipped and assured, and sipped more tea.

"Stuff that!" A tear sprang to my eyes.

"Caro, really, I don't think you're in a fit state to talk to. You're agitating yourself and you'll be no good to the girls if you don't stay calm. They need you to hold it together, Caro."

"Did you touch them?"

"Caro!" He sighed heavily and leaned forward, holding my gaze, "You know we agreed years ago that our needs are not the same."

"Did you touch the twins?"

"Of course not. I don't know how you could ask such a thing."

"And the others?"

"Caro, we agreed."

"But..." I started to sob, "I didn't know..."

"Didn't know what Caro? We agreed to have a community that would be perfect for everyone. Indigo and Xanthe's needed other soul goddesses to grow up with and we could meet the needs of those who joined us. It was the best place for everyone. I stand by that,."

"What are you saying?"

"That I only met the girls' needs."

Lynne came over and squatted next to me. She had on the same green jumper that she always and misshapen dungarees. "Stephen's right, Caro," she cooed. I noticed how her crooked teeth seemed to have yellowed more. "He was their safe pair of hands. Children are so sexualised these days."

"I'm not sure I understand all this. Why are they making accusations if…? "

"Because Bethan has got the wrong idea and blown it out of proportion and is dragging Juliet along with her. Bethan's been a loose cannon since she moved. It was a hostile gesture to the community, moving out of the area Bethan used to be so willing to learn, but she's changed. I've worried for years about her bad influence on Ceridwen."

"Did Xanthe see you with Freya?" I blurted out suddenly.

"What?" Stephen's nostrils flared.

"She told me once. She walked in and you had your hands on Freya… but she was only eight at the time. I told her she must have seen it wrong."

"Good."

"But what if they question her, Stephen?"

"They can't," Lynne put in decisively. She straightened and walked across the room to stand behind Stephen's recliner.

"What do you mean, they can't?"

"They can't interview children without parental permission. If you don't give permission they might get

60

shirty with you, but they're toothless. There's something in the Children Act about getting an order to make children talk, but it's never used, it's pointless. Anything they get out of kids who are forced to speak won't stand up in court."

"You've been doing your homework."

She grinned and Stephen patted her hand.

"Is there anything else they could find?" I asked.

"This is going to be a dirty war, Caro. You've got to be prepared. They will twist anything they can. Social Services aren't interested in child welfare, just in dumbing us all down to their unsoulful level and keeping us on a leash. All I've ever done was to put the children's needs first, but these social workers and police won't see that. They're stupid, Caro and they'll damage the twins' souls forever if you let them get anywhere near them. There's nothing wrong with sexual expression. Children are sexual beings as well as spiritual, you know that. The harm is when it gets perverted into shame and fear."

Stephen took a breath and gulped down the last mouthful of his fruit tea. He looked flushed after his speech. At his side Lynne virtually glowed with admiration. She didn't need him to take her to bed, I realised. She could orgasm over his words.

I rang Juliet that evening, but she was icy and monosyllabic. I tried Bethan, but she treated me as though I was the guilty one. I could picture Bethan curled up on her expensive cream sofa in the plush living room of the house she bought about eighteen months ago.

"We only got back from the evidence suit half an hour ago. It's been a very long day," she said.

"Did they interview the children?"

"Yes."

"How could you let them?"

The girls wanted to, Caro. It was really hard, but it was a relief for them too. They've been amazing. Heloise is coming home tomorrow to give a statement." She paused and I wondered if she was drinking coffee, the rich strong Indian blend that she loves and that Stephen always denied me. "You know, I think Xanthe and Indigo would feel a lot better about everything if they talked to the police. They'd feel like they were standing with their friends, standing up against something wrong."

"Indigo and Xanthe don't have anything to tell!" I leaned into the paisley patterned wall for support, wishing Lynne would hurry up with the decorating.

"Don't they? Freya says Xanthe saw something pretty serious."

"Xanthe never saw anything! What did Freya say she'd seen?"

"How do you know she saw nothing, Caro, if you don't know what I'm talking about? Anyway, you know I can't tell you what Freya said, it would ruin the evidence."

"I just know! My girls aren't involved in this, any of it."

"Caro," she had that slick gentle voice on. It reminded me of the voice Stephen had used to soothe me into compliance. "Do you really think that? It's just... Well, it's suddenly horribly clear to me that this thing was... I suppose it was a whole culture of corruption that Stephen built up. I don't think the twins could have been there and not been effected by it."

"I don't believe that. And I'm not teaching them that their father is a pervert. Don't you ever dare speak to them about any of this!"

62

"It's not my place to question your children, Caro. You know me better than that..."

"I don't think I know you at all," I cut in, crying.

"I'm sorry, Caro. This is hard on everyone, but speaking out is something the children can do. Even if Stephen didn't touch the twins, he subjected them to an atmosphere where things were never what we thought they were. If they can talk about it, I think they'll start to heal, that's all."

"You sound like a social worker. My children are not going to be sullied by this. It's wrong!" I slammed the phone down and slid down the wall. All I ever wanted was to give my children a normal, happy childhood. How could it be too much to ask? I stayed there, until Indigo came out of the living room.

"Mum! Mum, what's wrong?"

I struggled up and wiped my eyes on my sleeve; a violet chenille sweater that I loved, though it had seen better days. "I'm okay, sweetie. It was just Bethan."

"Dad says Bethan's gone mad."

"I think he might be right, sweetie. I'm afraid some police might come tomorrow, but you don't have to talk to them."

"Dad says Bethan has made up loads of bad stuff and told Ceridwen she has to say it to the police. Dad said Bethan won't let Ceridwen see him anymore. And Juliet was in a really weird mood when she came for Freya and Caitlin yesterday. Dad said Bethan's got to her as well."

"I'm afraid so, darling."

"Why's she being like this, Mum? Will we be able to see our friends?"

"I don't know, sweetie. I'm afraid..." I choked again and Indigo came and held me tightly as Xanthe emerged from the living room. She stood and looked at us a moment and then joined her sister. My two angels held me tight while I sobbed. "I'm… afraid... the police… they might…" every word was a struggle, but I forced myself on, "they might have arrested your Dad tonight."

Indigo sprang back like someone had slapped her and Xanthe began to cry loud, retching sobs like a toddler.

"I hate Bethan!" Xanthe pronounced and ran upstairs. When her door slammed the whole house reverberated.

The police arrived the next morning, but at least the twins were out. Lynne came early to take them out for a day of shopping and to see a film. Gwen, the police woman, was tall with thin mousy hair in a wispy pony tail. She was just a girl in her twenties trying to tell me about children. The social worker, Pam, was all syrup coated threats, but I stood my ground.

"We understand from Ms. Prichard that her daughter made an initial disclosure about three weeks ago and that you were informed at the time. Is that right, Mrs. Beaumont?"

"I think she might have said something, but it wasn't very clear. She was very upset, not really making sense. I thought she'd had a row with Stephen. They were very close friends."

"So you weren't aware that there was an allegation of sexual abuse?"

I began to cry. I cried more than I'd ever cried in my life, so much that I could see the fear in their eyes. By the time the people with the tape recorder arrived, I was calmer, only occasional sobs bursting out. They explained everything to me very slowly; how they would interview me at home, how I was what they called a 'vulnerable adult'. At least that was the truth. At least these so called professionals could see what Bethan failed to see: if anyone was Stephen's victim it was me.

It was such a relief to tell my story. I told them everything. I told them about my awful childhood, about being abandoned by my mother and beaten by my God-fearing father, about getting pregnant and the abortion. I told them every detail of the awful years of living with Andrew, how I was not much more than his prisoner and how it had left me susceptible to being preyed on by someone charismatic like Stephen. I told them about the years of emotional abuse and having my life controlled, until in the end I was a prisoner in my own home. I confided that I was terrified that Stephen might come after me or even try to kill me and the girls when I moved out. I told them that I knew he cared more about other people's children than he did about me, but I'd never thought… and then Bethan said… but she was so unclear.

In the end Gwen asked, "Did you agree with Ms. Prichard that no children would be allowed to stay with your husband after the allegation had been made?"

I started to cry again, a soft whimper this time. Gwen reached out and held my arm, ignoring the look from the woman working the tape.

"I think we said no children would be left alone with him. I couldn't stop my daughters seeing their dad or having a birthday party. Stephen said it was just a misunderstanding with Bethan and she wouldn't really tell me anything and anyway Lynne promised to be always there."

"That's Lynne Waters?"

I nodded and caught the look exchanged between the two officers. Obviously they didn't trust Lynne.

"She's known the girls since they were born." I sniffed.

"But you didn't only leave your own children in the care of your husband? After the allegation, I mean."

"It was their birthday. I couldn't ruin their birthday. Only Freya and Caitlin stayed over and Lynne promised… I didn't know what else to do…"

I lost control again and Gwen patted my arm, "I understand, Caroline."

"Caro," I corrected, sniffing again.

"We really would like to speak to your children when they are at home. We can come back tomorrow. I can promise you we're very careful in how we talk to children. It's…" she looked at her notebook, "Indigo and …"

"Xanthe." I finished for her, seeing her screw up her eyes trying to read the name. "I really can't allow that."

"Maybe you would like to sleep on it," Pam put in.

She had sat quietly during my interview, but she stood up now, and walked towards the kitchen table where the recording equipment was perched and where I sat with Gwen and the other officer. Pam had one of those bad walks that fat people have when their legs chaff together and I thought she should use more deodorant.

"We do need you to tell your daughters why their father has been arrested even if they can't talk about it with us."

"No!"

"We'll come back tomorrow," Pam said, as though I hadn't spoken. "Will 10 a.m. be convenient?"

"I don't care what time you come, I'm not telling them."

"We'll say 10 a.m. then." She nodded towards the police officers and they both got up. The sour faced one began to clear away the equipment.

The next morning Indigo, Xanthe and I caught a 9a.m. train from Temple Meads to London to stay with a friend. I had to protect my angels.

Dear Ceridwen III

I wake with the journal open on my bed, a dream image of you still vivid in my mind. I can almost touch you as you sit at an easel in Nain's studio. Your tangle of dark curls falls across your face as you crane your head to one side, eyes screwed up and questioning, wearing one of Nain's oversized russet painting smocks, the arms rolled up and spattered with turquoise paint. I struggle to surface into the day. It is cold today. I can see the glare of winter sun piercing the curtains. The thought of the morning routine makes me dizzy; making fires that will warm only me, cooking food for one. I close my eyes, slip back into the groggy half world of dreams and self recrimination. Guilt is always the last thing I feel before falling asleep, the first thing I feel on waking.

'What's done is done, Bethan. The only thing you can change is the present, girl, and you can't do that in bed, look.' Nain's voice cuts through the haze of self-pity.

"Everything seems so pointless, Nain."

'It's never that, cariad.' Her voice softens from sharp slate to breakfast muffin.

"Really?" I feel a single tear on my face, a world's weight of grief in one drop.

'It'd do you good to let it out a bit, Bethan girl. You've got too much held in for your own good, if you ask me.'

"That's something Caro might say, Nain."

I feel a slap of indignation in the cold air. 'I'll thank you not to compare me to that one, Bethan Prichard. I'm not saying you should start flooding the world in tears to get your own way, now, but you can't bite it all down, either. Something will give, mark me."

I bury my head in the pillow and feel the physical jerk of the tears as they wrench all the way down to my gut. When the last sob subsides I feel Nain's hand. Paper dry, long fingers stroke the back of my neck for an instant. 'There now, light the fires, Bethan, and run yourself a bath while the place warms through. Dafydd'll be here by ten with the coal.'

I sigh and sit up.

'And don't you dare ask me what you've got to keep going for.' Nain puts in before I can raise any objection. Her voice is brisk again. 'I've told you she's not dead.' There is a pause that makes me lean forward to catch what she will say next, 'It's not over till it's over, Bethan. I didn't much care to get out of bed when your mam was taken, but there was you and Bryn to think of and if there hadn't been you and Bryn there would have been something else. That's what life is, Bethan, not giving in.'

I throw the duvet back, the pale blue outline of mountains screen-printed onto the white cotton, one of the many summer craft projects that Nain dreamt up for you. Nain is silent, but I can taste her approval in the crisp air as I breathe in and stretch. Later, bathed, fed and dressed to face the day, the stoves glowing, Daisy purring on the living room rug, I settle down with the journal again.

December 20th 2003
Dear Ceridwen

Golden days... Looking back with hindsight nothing is the same, Ceridwen.

The autumn you were seven you went into class two at the small school. It was the class where you would be officially taught to read in keeping with the quirky philosophy of the place, an idiosyncratic mixture of Steiner and New Age, though in fact you'd begun to read before you ever went to school. I didn't have Caro's zeal for the alternative philosophy of the school, but I was satisfied that you were happy as well as learning.

It wasn't only at school that you were making a transition. In Caro's parenting classes I discovered that you were entering a new soul age, moving out of the Magical Bond Phase and into the Intuitive Blossoming Phase. This was the age when the gurus of soulful parenting believed little goddesses needed a father's influence, though at this age a little went a long way, Caro reassured us. Sometimes Stephen would emerge from his study to join in one of your games or chat about the drawing you were concentrating on, your curls hanging like a shaggy mane, your eyes serious with the effort of getting some artistic effect that Nain had taught you.

We had Christmas with Nain as usual. Tŷ Gurig always had a particular attraction in winter, the lashing of wind and rain, the short days when the dark closed around us like a blanket, so that the stoves seemed all the more comforting and Nain's hearty food all the more fortifying. Nain was good at feasts and untroubled by mess. She baked mountains of mince pies; let you roll out the rich short crust pastry or spoon the spice scented mixture into trays. She chopped and browned and rubbed and tasted, concocting game pies or carefully unwrapping thick slabs of fruit cake to add extra brandy while you spread a treasury of glitter, metallic paints and snow spray across the sheets of paper laid out on the huge pine kitchen table.

We had an extra treat that year: a visit from Bryn. We hadn't seen him since his fleeting visit to do some research at the Bodleian when he'd helped us move into our new home in Bristol. It was even longer since we'd seen his American wife, Mary, and their son Gethin, named for our Grandfather.

"Gethin, draw me a deer." You commanded, delighted to have a big cousin to attend to your every whim.

"Please could you draw me a deer, Gethin?" I corrected, smiling. I remembered how I had idolised Bryn as a child, how excited I was whenever he was due to come home from Oxford for a vacation, how I would pester him to play with me or assist me with some adventure that required a big person.

"That's alright," Gethin said, smiling back at me. "No problem, Ceridwen. Is this a big shiny nosed deer or one of the little followers?"

"A running deer, a fast one. Here. Draw him here."

"Your cousin is a very patient young man, Ceridwen Prichard. One more deer and then I'll run you a bath." I watched the colour rise in Gethin's fourteen year old face as he hunched in closer to draw the deer. He had Bryn's gangling length and mousy hair, blue eyes more deeply coloured than Bryn's, taking their cue from Mary, and her fair complexion that turned easily to pink.

"With Nain bubbles?"

"Yes, with Nain bubbles."

"And hot chocolate after, with cinnamon on the top?" You wrinkled your nose to concentrate on pronouncing 'cinnamon'.

"Well..."

"You can help me make it when you're in your pyjamas." Nain put in, tucking the next tray of mince pies into the oven and winking at you.

It snowed briefly at New Year, but when we arrived back in Bristol the streets were slush covered and disheartening.

"I miss Gethin," you said as soon as we piled our travel bags into the hallway, "And Nain," you added loyally.

"I know, love. Me too. We'll talk on the phone soon and you can put up the pictures that you and Gethin did."

We settled back into our life of school and work. It was a Saturday towards the end of March when Caro phoned so full of fitful tears that I could hardly understand what she was saying.

"Bethan, Bethan I need to stay with you tonight."

"Caro? You sound awful. What is it?"

"Stephen. He's… I can't talk about it… I can't believe…"

"Caro, tell me what you need. Take a deep breath. Is Stephen hurt?" My mind raced to freak accidents, though Stephen didn't seem to leave the house often enough to collide with a car.

"Hurt?" Caro shouted so loud that my ear pulsed with pain for a moment. "Bethan, this is about me!"

"I'm sorry, Caro. I'm just trying to make sense…"

"Swine!" Caro was always careful with her language, not only in front of the children, but in case she should coarsen her own soul.

"Stephen's done something?"

"I don't know how he could be so disgusting. It's vile. There are worms with more taste and decency."

"Do you want to tell me about it, Caro?"

"He… the filthy… God, Bethan. I'm beautiful. I am beautiful, aren't I?"

"You're lovely, Caro, but I don't…"

"And she… she's…" Caro broke down into wordless sobs while I began to put the pieces together.

"Is Stephen having an affair with someone, Caro?"

"An affair?" Caro's voice rose shrilly again. "Don't dignify it with words like 'affair', Bethan."

"Right. And you know the other…"

"Know her? I share my life with her."

My mind raced. Surely Juliet would never… Rachel?

"Bitch!" Caro sputtered, "Nasty, dumpy little bitch!"

Lynne? My mind reeled. I'd wondered sometimes how Stephen and Caro had ever got together. Plenty of average looking men seem to find beautiful women, but it was not only that Stephen lacked distinctive looks, apart from his startling blue eyes, more that he seemed to be one of those men peculiarly lacking in anything that resembled sexuality. He simply failed to give out the slightest chemical spark. It was something that I'd remarked on to Juliet. She joked that she thought he was a closet gay, an opinion she'd formed watching him whenever his old school friend, Matt, visited. Juliet and I decided that what must have attracted Caro to Stephen was not physique, but his confidence, his ability to charm or convince. We guessed that, Stephen, for his part, was delighted to have a wife who looked the part of a grown-up soulful goddess. It had always been clear that Lynne was besotted, but I would never have imagined Stephen favouring her with more than an occasional smile.

"Are we talking about Lynne, Caro?"

"Who else looks like the back half of a goat and has the morals of a dog?"

I took a deep breath and decided not to take the bait. Caro was upset and not herself, I told myself.

"Caro, why don't you come over? The futon makes into a decent bed. I can cook you something while you take a long bubble bath and you can get a good night's sleep."

Caro began to cry again, a strange whimpering sound that gave me gooseflesh.

"Caro?"

"You're so kind, Bethan. I can't believe he would do this to me."

"I know. Come over. Come straight away."

"I will." Caro sniffed and the phone went dead.

Caro was as tearful the next morning.

"I'm sorry I haven't got any vegan margarine in," I apologised, trying to attend to the practical things and hoping to distract Caro before you came into the kitchen and began asking questions.

"Really, Bethan! How many times do I have to tell you how evil dairy produce is?"

"Well, you know me, always living on the edge."

"I'm serious. It's not just your body, Bethan, it's your soul too..." Caro broke down again as you wandered in, rubbing sleep out of your eyes.

"Why's Caro sad? Who made her cry?"

"Caro had some bad news, love. Would you like a bagel? I bought them yesterday from Milly's."

You nodded emphatically. "Cream cheese and bacon," you added, a new favourite after your cousin Gethin had introduced you to this delicacy at Christmas.

Caro looked up and wiped her eyes. "You don't let her eat bacon as well do you?"

"Oh, Caro, worse things happen at sea, my dear." I tried to sound light, but Caro looked resolute, determined to argue about everything.

"Why don't I take your coffee through to the living room for you? You can have a nice peaceful start to the day while I get Ceridwen sorted out." I picked up Caro's brimming mug of coffee, a forbidden substance in her own home, and steered her out of the kitchen.

"Do you have to go to work today, Bethan?"

"I'm afraid I do. Juliet is doing the school run today. Then…"

"Oh God!" Caro sank onto the sofa that was still made up as her now unkempt bed. The air of the living room had a stale, sweet odour. "My poor babies! My dear, sweet, precious girls. How will they survive waking up without me? Not knowing where I am?"

"I'm sure Stephen…"

"Don't even say his name!"

I thought of asking her to talk quietly so that you wouldn't hear anything in the next room, but decided it might only provoke more of an outburst.

"Caro, I've got to get Ceridwen some breakfast. I know all this is terrible for you, but Juliet will pick up Indigo and Xanthe as normal and that will give you a day to do some thinking. I'm just next door if you need anything."

I inched out of the living room and headed back to the kitchen. You had already put bagels on two blue plates and were rummaging in the fridge for cream cheese and orange juice.

"Thank you, Ceridwen. Can you pass me the bacon too?"

You handed over the pack and stood next to me while I set it on the oven. "What was the bad news? Did Caro's Mummy die?"

"No, love, nothing like that. Caro just had a friend who... well sort of let her down and it made her feel sad.

Sometimes people do things we don't like, they upset us and it makes us want to cry."

You nodded. "Yes."

That evening, when you were in bed, the twins tucked onto a mattress on your floor, Caro sat at my kitchen table eating dhal and mushroom curry and worked her way through several large glasses of red wine.

"She blackmailed him, you know," she pronounced halfway through the second bottle.

I smiled, not sure how to answer, thinking it would be better to simply let her talk.

"It's the only way he would sleep with a dumpy little gnome like her."

I smiled again.

"Are you listening to me, Bethan?"

I winced at the tone of uncharacteristic belligerence and hoped she wouldn't get loud enough to wake you and the twins, especially as Xanthe had gone to bed so reluctantly and only after Caro had encouraged her to give full vent to her feelings on the subject.

"Of course I'm listening. I just didn't want to butt in while you were talking."

She looked mollified, took another gulp of wine and continued, "She has something on him and that's why he agreed to shag her. So she wouldn't tell."

"Caro! What on earth could Lynne have on Stephen?" I laughed nervously, unsure of what revelations the next swig of wine might produce, "He hasn't been defrauding the tax man has he?"

"You don't know the half of it. You're so trusting."

Caro spoke in a fast, tense clatter like rain before thunder. Her eyes were moist with the constant threat of tears and unnaturally shiny from the wine. She rested her head on the table for a moment, sat up and forked some dhal around her plate without eating it.

"Poor trusting fool, Bethan," she said in a sing-song voice and then laughed; a loud, harsh tone that reminded me of hyenas on wild-life documentaries. Making mischief, I thought, with Nain's voice in my head.

I decided it was the drink talking and shepherded her to bed in the living room.

"He shagged her to keep her quiet," Caro insisted again as she pulled the spare duvet around her.

I went back to the kitchen to fetch a jug of water and a glass, hoping it might stave off some of the hangover Caro would have in the morning. She was already asleep by the time I got back to the living room. I set the water on the coffee table and tiptoed out to the sound of Caro's snoring.

I washed up in the kitchen, weary, and sank into bed without bothering to shower. I wondered if Stephen was up to some dodgy dealing, but nothing more.

Caro and the twins were with us for less than a week, but it felt much longer. Caro became a walking tear drop leaving a trail of used wine glasses, bathroom towels and dirty clothes the way a snail leaves slime. I felt irritated and out of sorts every time I opened my own front door, snapping at you when I should have been insisting Caro clean up after herself and her girls. You were just as put out, impatient with the twins' disregard for your pristine little bedroom.

"Ceridwen, sweetie, you have to understand that Indigo and Xanthe have been through a lot this week. It's really not fair to bully them over a few toys and clothes when we're all so sad. It's very selfish, Ceridwen. The twins are much younger than you and very sad. You should say sorry for upsetting them like this."

I heard Caro's lecture as I walked upstairs after work. I'd been leading a workshop on therapeutic journaling for a group of refugees still struggling with English and I was drained. I couldn't hear your reply, but I caught the note of strained indignation in your voice, the quaver that signalled the onslaught of rare, but earth-moving tears. I marched towards your bedroom, steeling myself to confront Caro, but was waylaid by another voice below me.

"Bethan, could you come down a moment? I really need to talk to you."

Stephen was standing in my hallway, hands on his bony hips, his sharp blue eyes dulled and red rimmed.

I froze for a moment.

"I'm still waiting for an apology, Ceridwen." Caro's voice commanded.

I left Stephen looking plaintive and bounded up the remaining stairs.

"Ceridwen doesn't need to apologise for letting the twins know how she wants her own bedroom treated." I spoke rapidly. "Indigo and Xanthe, you need to clean up in here before you go."

It was the first time I had stood up to Caro and I was shaking. Caro opened her mouth, thought better of it and began to cry.

"Caro, Stephen is downstairs. I think you need to talk to him and decide what you are going to do next," I persisted, trying to keep my voice steady.

"You want me to leave?" The tears halted abruptly. Anger flashed through Caro's grey eyes.

"No, I want you to start to think about what you want to do. Ceridwen and I can't be more than a stop gap, Caro."

Caro turned and stalked downstairs.

"Now girls, your mummy and daddy need to talk down there. I'm going to cook some supper for us all and while I do you can get this room looking tidy again. Ceridwen will show you where everything goes."

Indigo started to whimper, "I can't... I can't... I want Mummy."

I knelt down and put my arms round her. "I bet you're brilliant at putting things away, Indi. Would you like some chocolate so you've got lots of energy for the job?"

Indigo wiped a delicate hand across her eyes and nodded. I pulled a bar of expensive organic dark chocolate from my work satchel, ignoring the voice that told me Caro would not approve of chocolate before dinner.

"How about you, Xanthe?" I held out four squares of chocolate, but she crossed her arms and planted her feet apart in determination.

"No."

"Okay. So which toys are you going to put away?"

"None."

"That's a shame, Xanthe. I'm not sure Ceridwen will want to let you play with her things again, in that case."

She flushed pink, but bit back tears and stood her ground. "Okay, Ceridwen, you and Indi see what you can do before dinner."

You smiled back in agreement and Indigo nodded vehemently, chewing on the chocolate.

I shut the door on the three of you and sank down onto the top stair, the fatigue of the week and the futility of arguing with six year olds congealing around me. I reassured myself that at least I'd mollified two out of three children and at least I'd made it clear that you did not have to be at the beck and call of these tyrannical little visitors. I unfolded and dragged myself towards the kitchen.

As I passed the slightly open living room door, Stephen came out into the hallway again. "Bethan, do you think you could come in here? We really need a mediator for this."

I could hear Caro crying loudly through the door. My head began to ache.

"Stephen, I'm sorry, but the girls are hungry. I have to cook something and to be honest I'm pretty starved myself.'

Stephen smiled thinly and put a hand on my arm, "Bethan, Bethan you are concerned with so many things, but sometimes the work of the soul has to come first."

I shot him a withering look, "I wasn't brought up particularly chapel, Stephen, my Nain was too maverick for that, but I know when someone thinks he's Jesus Christ and frankly it's not impressive." I was aghast at my own audacity, especially so soon after challenging Caro.

"I only meant…"

"Stephen I'm tired, I'm thirsty, my house is a mess, which really rubs me up the wrong way, and I have three hungry children upstairs, all of them pretty upset and confused and two of them your responsibility. If you and Caro can't talk without me, you'll have to sit in silence till after we're all fed and watered. I'm sure Caro can keep crying till then."

I regretted the last sentiment, or at least saying it out loud, but Caro probably didn't hear over her wails. It was the longest speech I'd ever made to Stephen and I watched his eyes widen as I spoke.

He nodded. "Loud and clear, Bethan. And thank you for taking care of them all week. I do appreciate it." He pulled a hand through his mousy, prematurely thinning hair and shuffled back into the living room, hands in the pockets of his expensive linen chinos.

In the kitchen I put on Radio 4, taking a school-girl satisfaction in an hour of news that Stephen would disapprove of me listening to within ear-shot of children. I chopped plump purple aubergines and glossy green courgettes and set a ratatouille sizzling while I measured out rice, refilling my coffee cup twice while I worked.

Dinner was a strained affair. A now taciturn Stephen and wan Caro moved food around their plates without appetite. You and the twins ate in watchful silence. I insisted on a proper bubble bath and story time for the three of you, determined to keep up my image of putting you first and equally eager to stave off what I anticipated would be a long night ahead of me.

I can hardly remember the conversation, except that it was endlessly circular and tearful on both parts. I occupied an uneasy position as advocate of both parties when all I wanted was to have my house back. Stephen tried to rationalise the affair away for the first couple of hours, endlessly repeating some variation of his own idiosyncratic version of fidelity, which apparently had nothing to do with who he slept with. I began to think I'd be there until morning, but Stephen thankfully tried another tack.

"Lynne left today," he said quietly, head in his hands. He was hunched into my little red sofa, picked up at an antiques market in Clifton. Caro and I sat across the coffee table from him on the futon that had been Caro's bed for the last week. It sagged on its frame and her bedding was scrunched down one side.

"Left?"

"Yes. She won't be coming back."

"Where's she gone?"

"She's got a cousin in Liverpool. He thinks he can get her a job in a housing co-op he's done some work for."

Caro smiled. She sat up, alert, her familiar erect posture and expansive gestures forming around her again.

"She coerced you into it, didn't she?"

My skin prickled, "I'm sorry, you two, but if you're going to be talking about things I don't want to hear, perhaps I'd best go and put a kettle on."

Stephen smiled. He looked suddenly confident again. "That's alright, Bethan. You've been great. Thank you. I think Caro and I should go home. Juliet will pick the girls up for school in the morning."

Stephen stood up and Caro followed. She leant over me where I was still perched on the futon and wrapped her long, elegant arms around me. "Thank you." Caro let one graceful tear slide down her cheek, pecked me on the cheek and thanked me again, more effusively now as her mood slid effortlessly from maudlin to upbeat.

So Caro and Stephen went on as usual. Caro sometimes lamented how impossible it was to cope with two children and a house without Lynne there to help her, but Rachel spent more and more time fulfilling Lynne's duties.

A few months after the reconciliation, Caro appeared one evening, looking her most statuesque and waving airline tickets. "It's to say thank you." She oozed delight.

"Caro, what do you mean?"

"They're for you and Ceridwen. Two weeks at a villa in Italy in July. Ceridwen will have to miss the last couple of weeks of term, but they're winding down then anyway. The place is absolutely gorgeous; olive groves and its own pool and the most stunning views you can imagine."

"Caro, it's too much. I mean I'm not sure we can accept something so big. We only put you up for a week."

"Nonsense, it's all settled. The tickets will be wasted if you don't accept. You wouldn't want that, would you? Ceridwen will adore it."

"You're very kind, Caro. I hardly know what to say."

"You only need to say yes. It's our thank you and you deserve it."

"Well, I don't know about that, but alright, yes."

Caro flung her arms round me and pulled me close, making me aware of how small I was in comparison and dousing me in her customary perfume, a mixture of ylang-ylang and something spicy. She stepped back and brushed a hand down her indigo velvet tunic that folded softly over familiar white silk trousers. "I'm so pleased. Indigo and Xanthe will be thrilled at having Ceridwen to play with on holiday."

"Sorry." I blinked stupidly, trying to catch up.

Caro smiled indulgently, "The girls, Bethan, they'll be delighted that you're coming with us and of course Stephen and I are ecstatic about it too. The thought of a holiday with no one there to lend a hand with the girls is just too exhausting. Lynne will never know just how much damage she's done."

"You mean we're going on holiday together?"

Caro laughed out loud and put a hand on each of my shoulders, "Of course, sweetie, you don't think we'd abandon you to a holiday all alone do you? What fun would that be? I have to dash now, but we'll have a proper chat soon. Of course it will be heavenly having someone along who appreciates the importance of soulful parenting, but I won't take a thing for granted. I'll make sure I go over every little detail so you know just how to treat my precious angels."

Caro swept out, the air still vibrating with her scent and energy, leaving me standing in my kitchen, mute and uncertain.

The villa was beautiful. A wrought iron spiral staircase rose from the open plan living area toward a mezzanine floor. Caro wandered around every room exclaiming on its loveliness.

"Just perfect," she pronounced when she returned to the seating area where all our cases where piled. "There's a darling bedroom for the girls with bunks and a single bed. I had them put in the third bed especially, but you should make sure Ceridwen has the top bunk. It might not be safe for my angels."

I stretched out on a long pale sofa while Caro continued. "The bathroom's so pretty and our bedroom is just heavenly. You won't believe the view. You must go up and have a look, Bethan."

"And I'm sleeping...?"

"Oh, here sweetie. These sofas are divinely comfortable aren't they?" Caro giggled and sidled towards Stephen, "Bethan can be our own little Cinderella, can't she Stephen?"

"I don't have a bedroom?" I wished instantly that I didn't sound like a sullen teenager.

"Bethan, sweetie, you won't need one. You're always up first and in the kitchen before anyone else and these sofas really are good. Don't you think?"

I knew it was futile to argue.

The first argument came after you demanded that Xanthe give you back your favourite night time toy; an old dog that had been mine as a child. Its white fur was aged to grey, but the black velvet ears were still soft and smelt of Nain's house. The next came when you adamantly refused to play the same skipping game for the thousandth time that day, biting back tears as you controlled your voice, "I'm too hot, Mummy and I'm bored. I want Indi and Xanthe to leave me alone."

Both times I managed to slip under Caro's defences and avert conflict. But on the last day your temperature shot up. I spooned liquid paracetamol into you, ignoring Caro and Stephen's disgust that I should even have such a thing with me. I constantly asked you to look at bright lights, checked that your neck wasn't stiff a million times over and scoured your skin for tell tale signs of disaster. By evening, you were cooler and fell asleep early. I negotiated with Indigo to swap beds with you, cutting Stephen and Caro out of the loop, aware that Indi would be the most likely to respond to my suggestion that she was being a kind and grown up girl to give you her bed at ground level for one night.

At bedtime I read extra stories to the twins, curled on Caro's king-size bed with the luxury view. When they were drooping with sleep I made a game of tip-toeing them into your room and tucked them in silently. Out on the landing I breathed a sigh of relief and headed down the cool open treads of the stairs towards a much longed for glass of wine. This time tomorrow we would be home. I told myself that soon you would be off to Nain's for the summer break and I'd join you for the last two weeks after the luxury of three weeks unadulterated writing time, a bonus of having a job that kept term times. Ten minutes later I heard you wail. I bounded up the stairs, maternal fear juddering through me, and flung open the door.

Xanthe was stood by your bed, her hand raised, her face screwed up and tear bloated. "She won't read me a story!" she shouted indignantly, "And Indigo wants her bed back!"

"Xanthe, stop that!" I shouted too loud. Caro was already behind me on the landing, but I continued, trying to regain some adult control. "Ceridwen is too poorly to read to you and Indigo is fine in the other bed." I tried to moderate my voice as I spoke, but I could hear its harsh edge. You were sobbing, your face flushed with exhaustion and fever. From behind me Caro pushed into the room. I watched her take a deep breath, fill out her height and glare at me as though I had three heads.

"Bethan, really! It's no wonder Ceridwen can be so selfish and unsoulful sometimes if that's the kind of example you set. Indigo is far too little to sleep on a top bunk. Ceridwen was fine this evening. She's just keeping up being poorly for the attention. Deceit is something that eats the soul away, Bethan, you shouldn't encourage her. I'm sure it wouldn't hurt her to read one little story. Can't you see how distressed Xanthe is?" Caro turned to Xanthe and scooped her up, "Mummy hears you, sweetie. You're feeling very hurt and angry at Ceridwen right now."

From Caro's arms I caught a glimpse of Xanthe pulling out her tongue, but I seemed to have lost the ability to breathe quick enough to interrupt Caro's righteous indignation.

"This isn't the first time I've had to speak to Ceridwen about her little acts of selfishness, Bethan. Really you must..."

You were ahead of me, "Shut up! Shut up and leave my Mummy alone! I hate you and I hate Stephen!" I winced at your vehemence, but I was damned if I would correct you.

I stepped towards you and put a hand on your forehead. "I'll need to get Ceridwen some more medicine now that Xanthe has made her ill again, Caro." I resisted the temptation to admonish Xanthe directly, telling myself to keep to the moral high ground. "As for selfishness, you've absolutely cornered the market there. If this holiday is your way of saying thank you for putting up with your endless self obsessed crying for a week, then I can only conclude that you are the most ungrateful person alive. Ceridwen and I came as your guests, not as slaves to replace Lynne. Come on cariad."

I held out a hand to you and scooped up your bed cover to take downstairs, where I spooned more paracetamol into you. I tucked you onto the second sofa with Snowdrop the dog tightly clutched to you, and stroked you to sleep. I was aware of Stephen hovering on the landing, listening to what was said in the bedroom, watching me comfort you to sleep, but he made no comment.

Caro waited until you were asleep and crept down.

"I think we need to talk, Bethan."

"No, we don't. I don't. I need to sleep, that's my need and my daughter's need." I shook as I spoke, but steeled myself to stay defiant.

"Bethan…"

"Go away, Caro." I rolled over, burying my head almost entirely under the covers. She hovered for a while and took breaths as though she was about to speak, but finally wandered back to her room. I drifted to sleep rehearsing arguments with Caro in my head.

Caro III

Stephen always said that the Universe holds a mirror up to our lives. I've always believed that, but suddenly it's as though the images reflected back to me aren't mine, but everyone else's ugliness instead.

Justin said something very wise. We were just getting out of the shower at his place. It's such a luxury to get to London, to be out of the parochial little huddle of Bristol. Justin's place is delightful, small, but big enough for Dominic to stay over, now that he's divorced vile Victoria. The bathroom is all white, painted floorboards, white roll-top bath, white shower curtains, gleaming white porcelain, white tiles, white roman blinds. I adore it. Actually, I adore the whole place. It's so chic and quiet, so unlike the prison I've been cooped up in with Stephen for years and a world apart from the tatty dump I've been reduced to living in since I left Stephen.

Anyway, we were getting out of Justin's power shower, him wrapping me in a big fluffy white towel and leaning in against my back, so I knew we'd end up back in bed even though we only got up half an hour ago. That's the wonderful thing about Justin, he wants a real woman. He calls me his Viking goddess and he's not being sarcastic. He wants someone mature and real, not that I'm saying there isn't a hurt little girl inside me that needs nurturing too. It's just that there isn't a trace of him hankering after some nasty little school girl. He loves that I'm tall and that my breasts fill his hands.

As I was saying, we stood there and I leaned back against him, warm and wrapped up, with that first tingling heat beginning to prickle between my legs.

"Justin is it me? Is there something wrong with me? I mean everyone hurts me, maybe it's my fault."

He was already beginning to move behind me. I could feel the hardness beyond the towel.

"Of course it's not you, darling."

He moved harder, but I wanted to talk about this. I reached an arm back and stroked his neck, pulled his head to rest on my shoulder. "You don't think the Universe holds a mirror up to our lives?"

"Maybe it does." He began to nuzzle into my neck, but I couldn't leave it at that. 'Maybe it does' might mean I was to blame after all.

I twisted round and put both arms around his neck. The towel unravelled and fell to my feet. I smiled at his sharp intake of breath, but took a step back, "Maybe it is my fault. Is that what you mean?"

His blue eyes flicked over me, assessing whether he could leave this on hold. He reached around my waist and pulled me back in so that I could feel every curve, his soft and hard surfaces rippling along my own. "Maybe what's in the mirror, Caro, is a person so giving, so loving, that bad people abuse her generosity. Maybe they mistake your big-heartedness for an invitation to trample on you. What you need is someone who wants all that love, but respects your needs as well. You're so complex, Caro. You're my strong Viking goddess, you're the nurturer and you're my needy girl who deserves to be loved and loved."

It all made sense then, as he reached both hands to cup my breasts and began gently twisting each nipple. He smiled, turned me around and moved his hand back to my nipple, teasing and twisting; the pleasure almost painful. His other arm pulled me to him tightly; his whole broad palm spread between my legs, playing me till I couldn't breathe.

So that's it, I thought, as I stood for a long time under the almost scalding water. I towelled slowly, rubbed thick organic body lotion into my thirsty skin and listened to the distant sounds of Justin cooking Thai noodles and vegetables in the chrome and white kitchenette where all the utensils were still new and shiny. So that's it – the Universe is holding a mirror up to me after all; showing me that I am simply too giving, It all made sense. I'd always helped everyone, cared for their children, listened to their problems, taught them how to parent soulfully. I'd been there for them night and day. I couldn't imagine ever being anything but soft and giving, but I could see that I would have to be more discriminating about who I gave my love to.

Justin made love to me again that night, slowly. "It's so long since anyone's appreciated you, really seen you." He told me.

He was so right. I deserved to be loved. It was Stephen who was the guilty one. None of this was about me.

Justin sympathised over breakfast the next morning. "That's the trouble with these people, Caro. They depended on you and didn't take care of themselves so now they blame you." He reached for more fruit toast across the smooth white table.

I started to cry. I hate to cry, but sometimes it's impossible not to. Justin passed a crisp white napkin across the table,

"Don't upset yourself over them, Caro, they're really not worth it. I'll run you to the station when you're ready. My first client isn't till ten today."

I dabbed at my eyes and forced a smile, trying to find my strong-soul place. "I know," I nodded, "It's overwhelming sometimes, but I know it's about them, not me."

I never had a clue about Stephen. Of course there were little things, like the time when the twins were about seven, and Xanthe said something odd.

"Come on girls, we need to go next door. Mummy's got to catch a train to the big Soulful Parenting workshop in London. You can play with Freya and Caitlin until Matt comes in from work. He'll cook you some tea."

"I think Freya's disgusting." Xanthe said.

"Well, we all have disagreements with our friends, sweetie. You need to let Freya know how you are feeling and then you can work things out."

"I told her she's disgusting. I want to stay here with Daddy."

Xanthe had that resolute face on and I began to feel anxious that I wouldn't make the train.

"I hear what you're saying sweetie. It's very important to me, but at the moment my needs are to catch a train. Matt is going to drop me on his way to work and he needs to be at work on time. We have to think about everybody's needs, you see, sweetie."

Xanthe flounced into the living room and sat down heavily on the red cushion. "I'm not going to Freya's."

I followed her, remembering to smile. I knew that if I focussed on honouring her feelings my needs could still be met. I had to get to the conference. It was vital to all of us that I had my emotional energy recharged.

"Xanthe, the thing is, Daddy is writing and he needs quiet. I'm sure Juliet will help you and Freya to work things out. If Freya's upset you then it's very important

90

that she hears this and apologises. I'll have a word with Juliet for you."

"I wish Lynne hadn't gone away."

"I know, sweetie, we all miss her, but Lynne had her own needs, angel."

"I don't like Matt living here."

"But darling, you adore Matt, you know you do and he's part of the family now. I don't know how we'd have managed if he hadn't joined us and you get to have Alicia around all the time. You love Alicia."

"This is our house. Me and Indigo are the children here. Alicia should live next door like the others."

"I hear that, sweetie and of course no one is as special as you and Indigo, but it's just the way things have worked out. We'll have a lovely long talk when I get back, but right now Matt and Alicia will be down any minute. You and Indigo and Alicia need to go next door so that Matt can take me to the train. I understand if that makes you angry or you need to cry or scream, sweetie. I think perhaps you need to let it all out, but I'll make sure Juliet has a word with Freya."

"No!" She was getting into her emotions now, which I could handle. I've never repressed my children the way some mothers do.

"I hear you, sweetie. Maybe you'd prefer to handle things with Freya yourself, but she's a bit older than you so if you need any help…"

"I'm not going to talk to disgusting Freya." Xanthe began to cry hot noisy tears. "Freya's a slut."

"Pardon?" I was shocked at the thought that my precious goddess knew such a word.

"Nothing!"

91

Xanthe stamped out of the room and pulled her coat off the hallway rack.

"Sweetie?" I felt sick. I was sure I'd miss the conference.

Xanthe wheeled round, tugging her coat on while Indigo stood mute on the stairs. "And he's my Daddy, not Freya's."

She sat on the stairs, sobs wracking her body. I peered up nervously hoping Matt and Alicia wouldn't hear. Xanthe stopped suddenly. "It was nothing." she muttered.

"Sweetie! Come here, let me give you a hug." She nestled into me, though she was never as soft as Indigo. I could always feel resistance in her. "I'm sure you're right, angel. I always misunderstand things when I'm tired or feeling low. Everyone does that. So you're alright with Freya then?"

Xanthe sniffed and raised her face, "Freya won't like me anymore. I told her she was disgusting and I hated her."

"I'm sure she's forgotten already, Xanthe. I'll tell Juliet you got a bit overwrought and can't even remember why and you didn't mean any harm. It'll all be fine. It was all over nothing, after all, right?"

Xanthe nodded. She was always such an honest child. She wouldn't have said it was nothing unless it was true.

Bethan twisted everything I told her. I could hardly be expected to think there was anything wrong with Stephen staying up at night. He had insomnia and there was nothing between us after that row about dressing up as a schoolgirl. He adored the children. He'd think nothing of staying up with them. He wanted to share their music, watch their videos, guide their choices, keep them on the goddess pathway. I suppose we never got to the bottom of that strange phase Alicia went through, but it was Matt we worried about, not Stephen.

Alicia and Matt came to live with us not long after Lynne left, and I have to say they were heaven sent. Matt had a job running a community project for children out of school, a bunch of disaffected kids over in St. Werburgh's. His job meant he wasn't as available as Lynne, but he had a car, which was a new luxury. He used to take the children on adventures at the weekends, little camping trips or kite flying on the Downs. Stephen had known Matt since schooldays at the Grammar School, though Matt had gone the more conformist route. He went to university rather than dropping out. His wife died of Hodgkin's when Alicia was three, around the time the twins were born, and he visited from time to time. Alicia attended the small school in Montpelier with all of our girls and was forever asking to sleep over, so it made sense for him to move in and we had more room with Lynne out of the picture, so that's how it happened.

Alicia was one of those goddess children who look doll-like. I used to think she was the fair version of Bethan's Ceridwen, except Alicia had finer features. She was, almost nine when she came to live with us, the autumn of ninety-five. She could be a strong willed little angel and sometimes I had to make sure she took the twins needs into account. Matt was a bit lax about the kinds of things she watched on video, which we had to be firm about, and the first year there was a silly incident when she jumped out on Indigo dressed as a witch at Halloween, not understanding that these frights can scar a young soul. But she grew enormously from being with us. It was lovely to see her blossoming as a giver. She soon learnt to put the needs of our younger little goddesses first and of course Xanthe and Indigo adored her once she settled in.

I was a bit surprised when I realised Matt was interested in Bethan, especially given the timing. Bethan was going through one of her wilderness periods, questioning everything, making all the wrong decisions and then Matt started mooning over her. Stephen was more philosophical about it. He saw it as an opportunity to bring Bethan back into the fold and make sure Ceridwen wasn't lost to us. He even asked me to go round to Bethan's and encourage her to see more of Matt. It wasn't an easy thing to do. Bethan and I had a terrible row at the end of the holiday in Italy. She spoiled the whole thing and I wasn't too happy about Stephen telling me to forget our differences, but I did go to see her and she started to see Matt.

It seemed like Stephen was right for a while. We had Ceridwen back on her soul path and Bethan seemed to be her old self again. Then Bethan suddenly broke it off with Matt and wouldn't talk about it. A month later, Alicia started having nightmares. The bed wetting was the most unsettling thing, especially in a child of ten. Matt insisted on taking her to the doctor, even though Stephen was against it. There was even an argument.

"For goodness sake, Matt, you can't trust your daughter to those quacks. She can see a homeopath. Caro has a friend in Clifton who knows Reiki. I'm sure we can handle this. It's an emotional thing. If you hand her over to quacks they'll make it worse. They're so crude and invasive, Matt."

"I don't want my daughter poked and prodded either, but what if it's physical? Do you know what it's like to loose someone you love, Stephen? I never stop thinking that if I'd noticed something earlier with Elaine... I don't know, something, anything, she might be here today."

"But this isn't like that, Matt. You're projecting. You have to stop and think."

"Look, I need to make sure it's nothing physical. I'm her father. I'm all she's got."

"We're a community here, Matt. You could be jeopardising all of us."

"I haven't a clue what you're saying, mate. How could I jeopardise you by finding out if my daughter has a bladder infection or, god forbid, a kidney problem or something?"

"Look, we're outside the mainstream. You're a single father living in a community. These people put two and two together and make guilty."

"Shit, Stephen, that's paranoid even for you. I'm taking Alicia to the doctor."

So he did and the quacks did exactly as Stephen had warned. They couldn't find a physical problem, but the consultant paediatrician had 'concerns'. Next thing we knew there was a case conference and talk of putting her on some kind of register.

"Caro, we have to stop this before Matt takes us all down with him." Stephen said to me one morning.

The children were at school and Matt was at work. I had whole days to meditate and find my strong soul place. I looked out into the garden from the big table at the back of our kitchen and said nothing.

"I think we should ask Matt to leave," he persisted.

"But you don't really think he's done anything to Alicia, do you? He's your oldest friend."

"I know. I'm gutted, of course, but I suppose it just goes to show that you never can tell about people. He's been through a lot, loosing Elaine and then everything that happened with Bethan. I don't want to judge him, but we can't risk him destroying everything. All these children rely on us, Caro. Their souls are our responsibility."

"Yes. Yes, you're right, but what if he won't go?"

"If he won't go I'll say we're going to make an allegation."

"Stephen!"

"It won't come to that, Caro. He's not stupid. He's already been through the mill with social services. He knows they'll seize any chance. If we say anything against him he knows he'll lose his job as well his daughter."

"But we wouldn't really make an allegation. It seems so brutal. Alicia could be put in care."

"It won't come to that, but we have to make him leave. It's the only soulful and moral thing to do, Caro. He brought this on himself. I knew Alicia didn't need a doctor. I warned him he'd be opening a can of worms. If we don't act they'll soon be investigating the other children; *our* children. If he goes we can say we weren't happy with him, that we didn't have anything we could quite put a finger on, but as concerned parents we couldn't take any chances with our daughters. We have to protect the other children."

As it turned out, Stephen didn't even have to ask. Matt announced next day that he'd found somewhere for him and Alicia to stay while they found a place of their own. A few months later Matt got a job in Newcastle and was gone completely. I was worried how the girls would react when we told them that Alicia was leaving, but they handled it so well, my angels. Indigo hardly said a word, just nodded and went up to her room to play her violin. It was her new passion. All night I heard the same tune over and over, *twinkle, twinkle little star* scratched out patiently on the tiny instrument.

Xanthe looked upset, but then surprised me, "I don't care if she goes." She said it in that determined way. "Alicia is like Freya."

"You mean they're friends, sweetie. Do they leave you out sometimes? I think I can hear some anger about being left out. Is that right?"

Xanthe slammed out of the living room without another word. Children are so resilient. I hardly ever heard my angels mention Alicia again and I had to respect that this was their way of coping with loss.

Of course, I did think that Stephen was a bit obsessed with Ceridwen. Truth be known, it was actually quite hurtful. That time I found him sobbing over Ceridwen, worrying that he wouldn't see her again was awful. It was only a couple of weeks after I'd moved out and I'll swear he never cried like that over me. He actually thought more of an eleven year old than of his own wife and all Bethan could think about was why I didn't suspect something. I was far too wounded to think about anything like that.

Dear Ceridwen IV

"I should have moved house straight after that awful holiday." I say out loud to Nain.

'You're too hard on yourself, cariad. You had your job. You and Ceridwen were settled. You had lots of friends there. All of them were just as involved with Caro and Stephen, more so even.'

I'm sitting on your bed talking to Nain. She decorated this room exactly as you wanted it, the long walls painted cream, the two end walls in deep purple, the colour so rich that I always feel as though I'll touch heather if I reach out. The long thin windows look out from two corners of the house, one towards the valley, the other towards the mountain face, your favourite view across the water fall.

"I don't want to give myself any excuses, Nain. I let her down. How could I not have seen anything?"

'No good will come of torturing yourself, girl.' Nain tells me practically, 'Blame's been allotted in the right place and you know that.'

"Maybe, but it's still so…" I struggle to find a less petulant word, but fail, "it's so unfair, Nain."

I curl onto the bed that has no scent of you remaining. The last visit was too long ago and the covers were washed, but the blue quilt is one that Nain made with you. Next to the bed, the windowsill is scattered with reminders, a piece of slate tile from the old outhouse roof, painted with Celtic knots; the scratch in the paintwork where you leant while you were drawing the waterfall. I let myself cry heavy, guttural sobs like a cow giving birth. There is no Nain to comfort me. Outside the steady thrum of rain turns to a torrent.

I wake next morning to the sound of insistent tapping on the front door, the noise gradually fighting its way out of my dreams. I shiver as I walk past the unlit stove, pull my dressing gown tightly round me and open the door a crack.

"Sorry to bother you, Bethan cariad." Dafydd's soft voice says in Welsh. I open the door a crack more and smile weakly, noticing the clock in Nain's open studio says it is ten-thirty. "I wondered if I could get you anything in town, like." Dafydd pauses to run a hand through the thin remnants of his hair and stoops his long back towards me.

"That's very kind. But I did a big shop a few days ago, thank you." I stop myself from saying that it was Nain who insisted I get dressed and get myself to the new supermarket full of glaring lights and harsh, festive music.

"I just thought, like…" Dafydd pauses to wring the cap that he holds uncertainly in front of him, "With it being Christmas and all, Eleri and me wondered if you needed anything and if you might want any company come Christmas day. But we'll understand if you'd rather not."

"Thank you Dafydd. You're right, I'm afraid, I don't think I'd be much fun and you've got all those grandchildren to entertain."

"Ah, I thought so, but I wanted to offer. You're always welcome you know."

I picture Dafydd's daughter Eleri in her busy kitchen organising a small army of her sisters, sisters in law and Dafydd's older grand-daughters into industrious Christmas work parties between rapid turns of bossing or fussing over the men. I can imagine the awkward silences that I would drag in my wake. "Thank you and say thank you to Eleri for me."

"Ah, I will, but if there's anything you need…" he leaves the sentiment hanging while he wrings his cap again as though to squeeze the last breath out of a suffering rabbit. "I've got a couple of trees left if you want one. I understand if it doesn't seem right, but maybe…"

He nods sympathetically, perhaps seeing the slight recoil of my body away from the notion of a tree, but behind me Nain whispers something in my ear.

"You know Dafydd, perhaps you're right. I didn't think I'd put a tree up, but then again…" the explanation won't come, but Dafydd nods anyway.

"I've got a nice one left that will do just right. I'll bring her round this afternoon, if that's alright."

"Yes, and thanks again, Dafydd."

I watch him walk away, the slow, slightly bent walk as though he is always carrying coal sacks.

December 22nd 2003
Dear Ceridwen,

Today I put up a Christmas tree for you. I cried over every ornament, every one a piece from my childhood or yours. I blubbed, counting the years in glass and metal memories…

The autumn after the awful holiday was one of the best times we had in Bristol. I was determined to put some space between myself and the community when we returned from visiting Nain, but surprised when you liked my idea of trying a new school. I was prepared for protests, but instead you hugged me.

Stephen and Caro were livid. "You can't possibly expose your little goddess to that place!" Caro wailed. I could see her picturing the local school and being careful not to mention that it had a rising population of Pakistani immigrants whose mothers sewed cheap t-shirts and badly cut jeans in poorly ventilated sweat shops.

"She'll be fine, Caro," I said, keeping up the pretence that her concern was for Ceridwen. "She's a very adaptable child."

"This is very spiritually immature of you, Bethan." Stephen said in a level voice. His sharp blue eyes fixed on mine. "This is like a teenager perpetrating some act of defiance out of chagrin when she knows she is only going to hurt herself in the end. We had a little misunderstanding on holiday, that's all. Now we need to move on, not punish our children for our failings. The community is very important to Ceridwen."

He paused and I wondered if he might be right. Was I being petulant or over-reacting? "You really have no right to uproot Ceridwen and trample on her soul like this."

"What?" My anger ignited again.

"Ceridwen is part of us, Bethan. She's not just part of some soulless nuclear family with only a single mother to shield her from the world. She's…"

"I beg your pardon? For your information, Stephen, my little family is not soulless and we're not dependent on you for permission to live our lives. Ceridwen is going to Baker Street Juniors this autumn. Now, if you don't mind I have additive-laden food and red meat to shop for."

I turned and stomped out. I slammed their front door behind me, relief surging in my blood like champagne.

You soon had new friends to invite for tea, Nisha and Sana, and I noticed that your friends from the community congregated more in our house now that I was an outcaste. I was relieved not to be cut off entirely, but I stubbornly refused to visit Caro and Stephen or go to Soulful Parenting classes, despite Juliet's pleas that the sessions were dull without me.

In October Matt moved in to Lynne's old room in the soulful living house and Alicia took over the remaining spare bedroom. I think Matt thought it would be good for Alicia to have some mother-substitutes in her life now that she was getting older.

"You have to come back to classes, Bethan. I'll die of boredom if you don't come and liven us up. Anyway, you can hang round the kitchen and watch the gorgeous, but lonely Matt cook. Maybe even invite him to dinner."

"If you think he's so gorgeous why don't you ask him to dinner?" I teased Juliet in return.

"Because I don't cook. Anyway I'm off men. You could ask us both to dinner if you want a chaperone," Juliet said, laughing.

The morning after Matt and Juliet came to dinner, Caro knocked on my door. She was wearing one of her familiar flowing violet tunics over white silk trousers. Her white cotton espadrilles gave her even more height so that I felt positively dwarfed as I opened the door.

"You met Matt?"

"Hello Caro. Do you want to come in?"

Caro waved aside the pleasantries and followed me into the living room. She eyed the futon as though it were an old enemy and plumped for the little red sofa.

"He's lovely isn't he? And he's been through such a lot. You'd be good for him, Bethan." Caro settled herself into a comfortable pose.

"He just came for dinner, Caro. So did Juliet. I wasn't thinking of picking out curtains with him."

"But you like him?"

"He seems nice. We have met before, Caro. He was at your house the first day I visited I think and I've seen him around the school or at your place occasionally."

"Are Alicia and Ceridwen friends then?" Caro smiled as though she were fitting puzzle pieces together.

"I think they hung out when they were in the same school and Ceridwen seems happy that Alicia is close by."

"That's good. Ceridwen certainly knows her mind when it comes to these things."

"Sorry, Caro, what things? Do you want a drink?"

"I'm fine thank you, just wanted to see how things went."

"And can I ask why all this interest?"

"Bethan, sweetie, you're my friend, and a very dear friend at that. I'm bound to be interested in your love life."

I choked slightly. "I'd hardly call one dinner with another friend present a love life, Caro, and I doubt Matt does either."

She looked exaggeratedly crest-fallen, her eyes mocking, "Oh sweetie, don't be such a kill-joy. It would be so good for you both. He's been alone for five years. Alicia needs a mother and Ceridwen needs a father. Really, it's perfect."

"Well that remains to be seen," I muttered, scrabbling for a way to change the subject.

Caro nodded, satisfied. "I must dash, sweetie, but I wanted to ask you to come to Soulful Parenting guidance tonight. We miss you ever so much."

"I... I'm not sure, Caro."

"Matt will be joining the group tonight. You can give him moral support and Ceridwen can sleep over with Alicia."

"I'll think about it."

"Good." Caro rose and swept out of the room, down the passageway and turned at the font door. "I'll see you at seven then, sweetie."

Why did I go? I suppose I was interested in Matt. I'd been single for a long time and now that I was over thirty I had a permanent suspicion that it was all downhill. I didn't only go for Matt. I missed the company of the group. I still saw Juliet, but I had hardly seen the others except to bump into Annette in the Asian vegetable shop, looking furtive and tired as she bought non organic broccoli.

"Do you fancy going to the community tonight and staying over love?" I asked when I picked you up from Nisha's house. The scent of spices sizzling in ghee made me suddenly hungry.

You waved goodbye to Nisha and we walked the two streets home, "No, I don't want to go there."

"Really?"

"I thought you weren't Caro's friend any more."

I laughed and squeezed your hand. "Well adults can't really stay not friends. It's grown up to make up."

"Did Caro say sorry?"

"Well, not exactly. but…"

"Anyway that's not true, Mum" I noticed how you said 'Mum' these days, not 'Mam'. "You're not friends with my Dad, are you?"

"Well, no…"

"So why should you be friends with Caro when she's not even sorry?"

We reached our front door and went in. You left your school bag on the hall floor and skipped along to the kitchen.

"Do you want curry? I've got some lentil dhal and mushroom curry made already and Nisha's Mum's cooking made me hungry for curry."

"Okay." You poured orange juice from a carton. "Will you cook chapattis? Can I help?"

"Okay. Let me put the rice on first. Do you want to measure out some chapatti flour for me?"

I waited until we were rolling out chapattis side by side before I raised the subject of the community again. "You're right about Caro, Ceridwen. She should apologise, I suppose, but it's not really in her nature and I miss my other friends and not being able to chat about things. I'd really like to go to the gathering tonight, cariad."

You paused from rolling a ball of chapatti dough in your hands and looked at me, your brown eyes appraising and serious, streaks of flour dusting your dark curls. "I don't want to sleep there, Mum."

"I'm not surprised really after the twins kept you awake like that when you were poorly."

You looked away and nodded, pounding the ball of dough flat with gusto.

"I think Caro realises you might not want to sleep with the twins, love. She says you can sleep in with Alicia. That would be fun wouldn't it? And I'll be there first thing to take you to school."

That was the end of my little rebellion against the community. You remained at Baker Street Primary, but otherwise life went back to normal. Do you remember kite flying with Matt up on the downs that winter? He had a stunt kite in luminous pink and green which would take ages to get airborne and then would soar, pulling us off our feet as we both struggled to hold on. You loved that feeling of the wind tugging us off the earth as the kite got smaller and smaller. Matt had a whole assortment of smaller kites, tough oblongs of rip-stop fabric in saturated reds and blues with wind sock spines in shocking yellow that would inflate as the kite pulled higher and higher.

"I love the wind." Matt confided. "When it's windy we encourage the kids in the project to stay indoors at break times. It seems to affect their mood. They get fractious and jittery like they're on something, but the buzz just does something for me. Clears me out."

He helped you unravel extra twine in a smooth movement so that your red kite rapidly became a dot in the clouds. "I'd better give Alicia and Freya a hand with the stunt kite before it pulls them off the ground." I moved with him. "We had a real windy Christmas the year Elaine died. I used to come for long walks up here. Me and the wind. I could wander round the Downs crying and howling and tell myself it was just the wind in my face."

It was four days before Christmas. We would leave for Nain's the next day. I gulped down Matt's sudden confidence, struggling to find the right words to reply.

"It's the anniversary of her death today. Six years. I'm still waiting for time to be the great healer."

"Right before Christmas?" I said stupidly, as though death usually declared a cease fire for public holidays.

"Sorry. I didn't mean to get maudlin on you. You just seem like someone I could..." Matt trailed away as we reached the girls. He deftly took the kite handles form Freya and then Alicia, relieving them of the fight with the stunt kite.

106

"Well done girls. Do you fancy a hot drink somewhere? We could wander down Whiteladies Road and warm up."

In the café we settled you, Alicia, Heloise and Freya along a row of high stools covered in red faux leather. You warmed your hands on tall mugs of hot chocolate, a delicacy that Juliet's girls were only allowed when Caro didn't know about it. The four of you sat and blew on the froth until the scalding heat had subsided enough to drink the thick, sweet liquid. Matt and I sat at a small table nearby with mugs of coffee.

"You drink coffee?" I asked.

Matt laughed. "I've known Stephen too long to be told what to eat and drink by him."

"And you're not a vegan?" I nodded towards Alicia's chocolate.

"Vegetarian with an occasional slip when the smell of bacon tempts me." He had brown eyes, not as dark as mine, the kind that seem to see humour in things. "So Bethan, all these questions. Am I being interviewed?"

I coloured and almost stood to leave, indignant and silly, but recovered. "You should be so lucky, Matt Ellis."

"Ah, shame. I thought I might have passed for a moment."

I did stand up then, pretending you needed me, and fussed over the temperature of your chocolate.

"It's fine, Mum. I can blow on it myself. Can we have biscuits?"

I took my time buying biscuits at the counter. I tried not to notice Matt watching me with an amused twinkle in his eyes. When I had no more excuses to hover over you I sat back opposite Matt and began draining my coffee cup as though it needed all my attention.

107

"Sorry, Bethan." Matt put a hand on my arm before I could lift the coffee cup to cover my face again. "I'm pretty out of practice with this stuff. I didn't mean to overstep..."

"No, you didn't. I mean... Me too. I broke up with Ceridwen's Dad when she was two."

"No-one since?"

I grinned. "Now who's doing the interviewing?"

"Touché! Well, seeing as we're both rubbish at this, I should probably stop going all round and the houses and just ask you out. You and me. No kids and no Juliet. What do you think?"

Before I could answer you called over from your stool. "Mum, are you poorly? You look all red."

Matt and I started to giggle together. "I'm fine, love. It was just the wind." I turned back to Matt and said quietly, "It's a date."

We spent the first few months sharing our ghosts. I felt as though I knew Elaine. She was the adult version of Alicia, pretty and bubbly and unable to believe that she could die. Matt told me all about the chemotherapy and the alternative therapy centre that Elaine had found, trying everything possible with unfailing optimism.

"I still can't eat a tomato without being back in that place. They had all these different theories about good and bad foods. Mangoes were good, tomatoes were bad. We were willing to try anything. Well, I suppose I wasn't up for Lourdes or Caro's mad friend from London who wanted to wave his hands over Elaine and extract her emotional malignancy. That pissed me off, but changing our diet didn't seem so unreasonable."

Matt had a way of sounding breathless when he talked about Elaine, as though he couldn't get the words out quick enough. He wasn't the only one who talked. He was the first person I'd ever talked to about Timothy. Even with Nain I was reserved. Nain guessed at the violence and told me he'd get what he deserved in the fullness of time, but she didn't pry. I'd always thought of it as a brief interlude that I'd got over quickly, but with Matt I discovered hidden reservoirs of hurt and it was a relief to drain them.

It was a slow relationship, both of us cautious and aware of you and Alicia stealthily watching our moves. Neither of us wanted to imply promises that we might not be able to deliver to our children, but despite ourselves we were soon taking each other into account in every decision. I noticed myself changing the bed sheets more often and buying more bacon than you needed to sprinkle on your cream cheese bagels. By the next Christmas we were a couple and Matt and Alicia even came with us to stay with Nain, braving Nain's unsubtle hints about marriage and not getting any younger.

The twins were seven that January and Caro hired a play centre that had once been a church hall to throw their party. She gave the catering staff careful and copious instructions. There must be no fizzy drinks, no food with colours, no dairy, no meat, of course. The bewildered cook produced plates of sandwiches with hummus and vegan cheese, a mound of vegan cakes that you complained tasted 'funny' and various carob and muesli deserts that went largely untouched.

While the children hurtled down slides into ball pools, Caro sidled over to where I was clearing a pile of plates.

"Leave those, Bethan, the staff can do that."

"I can't resist lending a hand I'm afraid."

Caro leant across the table to scoop up a glass and poured red wine from a bottle she had carried over. "Sit down and drink this, Bethan. We never get enough time to talk these days. You're so tied up with Matt."

I sat down, but ignored the wine. "I suppose relationships do take up quite a bit of time."

"So how is it all going?" Caro leaned too close so that I could smell the alcohol on her breath.

"Fine. Really good, I think. We had a lovely Christmas and..."

"Good, sweetie, I'm glad for you, really, but I do think you need to notice other things. To be honest my life's a mess."

"What?"

"If it wasn't for the twins I don't think I could go on. I need a life of my own, Bethan. Everything I do is for someone else. I'm always giving, but one of these days I'll need something back."

Caro drained her glass and poured another while I scanned the ball pool hoping to notice a child calling for attention.

"I don't know what will happen to us, Bethan. It's not as though I love Stephen anymore, but he's the father of my precious angels and he's so worried."

"Worried you'll leave him?" I ventured, perching on the edge of my seat for a swift get away at the first opportunity.

"Worried he'll go to prison, more like."

I sat bolt upright and stared, speechless.

"I can't really tell you what it's about, Bethan. He's never exactly let me in on our financial arrangements."

"So it's something to do with money? I thought Stephen inherited..."

"Like I said, I don't understand it all, but he could be done for fraud apparently. The important thing is that if he is done he mustn't take me down with him."

"But if you don't know…"

"Don't be naïve, Bethan. I'll be guilty by association, that's how these things work. Who would ever believe that someone could do these things and his own wife would know nothing? I mean under the same roof and all."

"I'm sorry, Caro, I must be being dense. I thought you said it was to do with money. What's he been doing under your roof exactly?"

"It's a figure of speech, Bethan. You are pedantic sometimes." Caro poured more wine and drank.

"Sorry, Caro, I think Caitlin has fallen. I'll just go and check."

It was a conversation I was keen to forget. Caro and Stephen's financial affairs were none of my business and anyway, as Caro rightly said, I was wrapped up in Matt. When I was first seeing Matt you were happy to spend nights over at the community house again, sharing Alicia's room, but after Christmas you became more reluctant to stay there. You and Alicia often pleaded to stay up till the class finished so that you could both come back home with me. Some evenings you simply refused to go all together so that my attendance at Soulful Parenting classes became fitful.

"Bethan, have you got a moment?"

It was a cold, grey March day, a Sunday I think. Stephen hovered on my doorstep, his face pale with the cold.

"Sorry, Stephen, come in." I led him to the kitchen and filled the kettle. "I've got some blackberry and apple tea if you want some."

"Please." He sat down at the table, unwound a plaid wool scarf and unbuttoned his black wool coat.

"So what can I do for you?" I loaded a tray with cheerful mugs, my coffee pot and a jug of milk.

"I'm afraid I need to talk about something rather delicate, Bethan. I think you should sit down."

I imagined he might tell me something like Caro had at the twin's birthday party, how he had financial problems and was uncertain what the future of the community would be. Perhaps he would even tell me that he expected to be arrested any day now and ask me to watch out for Caro and the girls. I sat down and braced myself.

"I'm afraid I've got some concerns about Matt, Bethan. I don't want to alarm you, but I'm really quite worried and it seemed only fair to warn you. I hope I'm wrong, I really do, and I probably am wrong, but I couldn't live with myself if I turned out to be right and I'd done nothing."

"I'm sorry, Stephen, I'm not following you."

Stephen momentarily put his head into his hands, sighed deeply and looked up at me. "You might have noticed, Bethan, that Ceridwen has been a bit... I don't know how to put this... I don't want to suggest more than... well, anyway, you've probably realised she doesn't like staying in our home as much as she used to."

"Well, yes. It's not the first time, but last time was after the holiday and I thought she was worried about the twins not letting her sleep. But yes, she has started to want to be at home at night. Actually, so has..."

"Alicia."

"Yes."

Stephen ran a hand through his thin hair and looked more anxious. "Look Bethan, this is just my gut feeling and I hate to be the one to sew seeds of distrust. Heaven knows, Matt and I have been friends since we were eleven, but... All I can say is I'm worried about him. He's been through a lot and I thought it would do him good to have you in his life, but perhaps its stirred things up that he can't control. I don't really know how these things work."

"Stephen! You're not making any sense." I could taste my own fear.

"I'm sorry, Bethan, really I am. To be honest I can't exactly put my finger on it. All I know is Alicia doesn't seem to be the happy little girl she used to be and now Ceridwen is frightened of being near Matt as well."

"Stephen! What are you saying? Ceridwen's not frightened of Matt. She's fine about him being around."

"Maybe he's more... I don't know... more cautious when he's in your place. God! I'm not even sure I should have brought any of this up. I could be over-reacting. The children all just mean so much to me, Bethan. Ceridwen's like one of my own to me."

"Stephen, do you have any... I don't know... not evidence exactly, but..."

"You know what an insomniac I am, Bethan. Well, I've noticed I'm not the only one who's up at night. Matt seems to be up a lot. You don't notice?"

"Me? I sleep like the dead, Stephen."

"Look, I'm probably way off the mark, but like I said, I feel responsible for Ceridwen. She's special. If I'm wrong, that's great, but I thought I owed it to you both... well... anyway..."

"Yes. Thank you." I stared out beyond the suddenly garish coffee mugs towards the grey sky and felt my insides freeze. Behind me I heard your tread on the stairs.

"I should go, Bethan. I'm really sorry."

We trudged to the park later, after I'd rung Matt to say I needed a bit of time alone with you. It was too cold to stay out for long, even the ducks on the lake looked as though they were shivering in the mean March light. I stomped over the thin grass past leafless trees, hands stuffed in the pockets of my blue duffle coat that seemed altogether too bright. I watched you run ahead, your thick curls streaming from under a rainbow woolly hat that Matt had bought you from a Latin American street vendor. Alicia had an identical one and you'd scrawled your initials unevenly on the labels to tell them apart.

Stephen was wrong, I told myself. But he was right about you not wanting to sleep in Alicia's bedroom. Back at home I made us hot buttered toast and filled the garish mugs with milky hot chocolate which we took into the living room to sip while we huddled together to watch your favourite video. Later, while you helped me roll pastry and whisk eggs for a quiche, I tried to quiz you without you noticing.

"So, are you sleeping over with Alicia on Wednesday when I have my group?"

"No."

"I thought you liked staying in Alicia's room."

"Caro's house is cold."

"I suppose they don't put much heating on when I think about it. Is that why you like to sleep here?"

"Yes."

"Nothing else?"

"No."

I took the coward's way out, Ceridwen. I told Matt that it was all too fast for me; too fast even though we'd been seeing each other for over a year. I told him I wasn't ready

114

for such a big commitment, that I was worried that soon you and Alicia would begin to see us as a family, would expect a certain future that I didn't think I could deliver. He looked bewildered and small while I spoke, but he didn't try to dissuade me. He didn't want Alicia relying on me if I wasn't going to be there for her, he agreed.

Stephen and Caro didn't say anything else. Instead they moved the time of the Soulful Parenting gatherings forward so that I could take you along and still be home in good time to have you in bed for school next morning. Annette complained that the earlier time made it hard for her to get dinner for Dave before she came out, but Caro brushed aside her objections with one of those sweeps of her arm and an acerbic little comment.

Matt didn't come to the gathering any more, but we bumped into each regularly, as I came or went, or when I was picking up your things to go home after you'd played with Alicia and the others. He was polite, in an awkward, slightly sad way, but nothing more. It was Caro, not Matt, who told me about Alicia's 'problems'.

"I realise you're not together, Bethan, but I know you're very fond of Alicia. We're just so worried about her."

"What does Matt say?"

"Oh, he's terribly blasé about it, Bethan. I'm really quite shocked. I mean a little girl of ten and a half really shouldn't be wetting the bed nearly every night. It's not normal. Matt says it's just a bladder infection and all he has to do is fill her full of poisonous drugs. Stephen's very disappointed in him."

"So Alicia is seeing someone?"

"The stupid G.P. couldn't find anything wrong so she's made a referral. She says it will be looked at as an emergency, which means it could still take four weeks to get an appointment with the paediatrician, apparently. I don't know how they can call that an emergency."

"But she is seeing a paediatrician?"

"Yes, though it won't do any good. This is a problem of the soul, Bethan. I can sense it. Alicia has some deep issue that she doesn't know how to work out."

It was June when Matt phoned to tell me that the paediatrician had expressed what he called 'non specific concerns' and that Social Services had paid him a visit.

"They're going to have a case conference, Bethan, I'm beside myself."

"A case conference?"

"Yes."

"So do they think...? I mean..." So Stephen had been right. I thought.

"Yes, they do think... or at least... I don't know, Bethan. I answered all their questions. I've never been so scared." Matt's normally steady voice cracked on the other end of the line, "I don't know how all this has blown up like this, but I can't lose her, Bethan, I can't. It's too much..."

"I don't know what to say, Matt." If there was nothing to find, then they would find nothing, I reasoned, but if they found something, if they suspected something...

I questioned you more that evening as you splashed in the bath. You gave no sign of hiding anything and I wondered if Stephen was wrong after all. I held my breath while Matt went through the ordeal of the case conference. Nothing was found, though Alicia continued to have nightmares and sometimes to wet the bed.

At gatherings I could sense people distancing themselves from Matt, mothers whispering to their children to play in Juliet's house or not to go into Alicia's room. Only Juliet was stalwart in her championing of Matt.

"I can't believe you, Bethan Prichard. Matt's the best thing that's happened to you in years. You can't seriously think he's guilty of anything?"

"I don't know, Juliet. I mean I've got Ceridwen to think of. It all seems so unlikely, but ..."

"Loads of kids go through weird patches, Bethan. God, the kid lost her Mum and then she lost you as well. Maybe that had something to do with it."

"No. I... I had some doubts before Alicia... I'm sorry, Juliet. I don't know what I think."

Juliet put a delicate hand on my shoulder. "I didn't mean to be judgemental, Bethan. I just find it impossible to believe."

"I know."

Within the month Matt had moved out and soon after that he moved to Newcastle. We didn't keep in touch.

Caro IV

When Stephen and I were first together it was a competition between us. It didn't mean anything. It was just a way of teasing each other, working each other up. We were young. Stephen still had that boyish face and my figure was stunning. He would pull girls at discos, young girls who lied about their age to get into night clubs and were after some no-strings-fun. Stephen didn't ask questions. Afterwards we would lie in bed in the pitch dark and I'd listen to his descriptions until we were both turned on. We made love like our lives depended on it on those nights. I preferred older men, the ones who looked like they could look after you, but might turn out to be a bit dangerous too. Stephen liked to hear about everything.

"People have fidelity all wrong," he told me. "They have this idea that they have to stop living, but that's not what it's about. Couples don't get jealous if their partner shares work or food with someone else, so why crack up if their partner sleeps with someone else? Real commitment is not having secrets, Caro. We have to tell each other everything: absolutely everything. Now that's fidelity."

I learnt so much from Stephen in those early days. Every day was an adventure and it was so refreshing to be with someone who didn't want to limit me. But somehow it changed after a few years. It rankled that Stephen went on pulling young girls, even though he wasn't getting any younger himself, while I was at home, bored. We only ever had sex after he'd scored.

"You do want me for myself, don't you Stephen?" I finally blurted one evening.

We started to row after that. We might have broken up if we hadn't met Lynne. She was living in the first Soulful Living Community House, a run down old Vicarage near Bermondsey Park that Ralph and Annabel were renovating with the help of the first community members.

Lynne introduced us to Ralph and we moved into the Soulful Living Community House. I knew Stephen was still pulling girls on the nights when he didn't come home, but at least he kept quiet about it. We hardly had sex anymore, but it seemed less important with the community around me. There were so many new people to learn from. Ralph was the wisest person I'd ever met and so generous. It wasn't as though I went to bed with him often, and it wasn't even as though the sex was the most important thing. He was my mentor. I wanted to learn everything from him.

Annabel never had Ralph's wisdom and I think she was jealous of what I had with Ralph, which was ridiculous. Obviously she had no understanding of true fidelity. I have a suspicion that it was Annabel that put it in Stephen's mind that he was ready to set up his own Soulful Living Community House. It was certainly Annabel who introduced Stephen to Clare. She was some sort of relative of Annabel's who had these two houses in Bristol that she was prepared to rent cheaply to a new cell of the community. So it was all set up. I was sorry not to be living with Ralph anymore, but it was exciting too. Stephen and I would be the Soul-Guides in the new community and I felt ready for the challenge.

We moved in eighty-five: me, Stephen and Lynne. It was September and I remember thinking that Bristol was a place where the rain never stopped. The houses were in a poor part of town with a lot of Asians and other people who seemed unlikely to appreciate Soulful Living. Clare said that a lot of young professional families were starting to buy first homes in the area and she'd bought the houses as an investment. In any case, money was too tight for us to have a choice about where to set up, though I often wished Clare's houses were in Clifton or Redland, where she lived herself.

At least the houses were a good size, not like the squalid little Victorian terraces around the corner in Easton. We faced out onto Eastville Park, part of a row of town houses that stood out from the shabbier neighbourhood. The two houses were identical: Victorian, red brick with square bay windows and three floors. Clare had done a lot of work on the houses. On the ground floor of each house there was a big square living room at the front looking out onto the busy road that ran in front of the park, a smaller room behind that and then a long kitchen-dining room.

In our house the top floor was our private space. We had the large bedroom, a bathroom and Stephen's writing room, which looked out over the small garden. Lynne slept in the room beneath us. Downstairs the living room was furnished with piles of cushions for meetings and the smaller living room was filled with crayons and toys bought from the Steiner shop on the Triangle in the city. We wanted to be prepared for the time when little souls would be a part of our Soulful Living House.

Ralph always says that the Universe has a way of making things come right if you are doing the right thing. We visited local toddler groups and community projects, put up posters in the library, and chatted to the lovely man who owned the whole-food shop, Harvest. He let us leave leaflets about Soulful Living, but we didn't attract many visitors at first. Life was unutterably slow.

"I know what we need to do, Caro." Stephen announced one morning at breakfast.

I looked up, waiting for his big idea. "I've been thinking about something Ralph said about the Universe honouring our focus. We're not making out intent clear enough. So I'm going to put things right. I'm going to commit myself to the new community with a period of celibacy."

"What?" Stephen went on eating his muesli as though he'd said something ordinary. I noticed his spoon had a brown tarnished patch, but didn't tell him. "You can't be serious, Stephen. We hardly ever do anything as it is!"

"It's not about quantity, Caro, it's about where my energy is focussed."

"It's me isn't it? You just don't want me. Now that you're not pulling bits of things from night-clubs in London, you haven't got anyone to work you up enough to want me!" My tears began to spill uncontrollably.

"Caro, you know it's not like that."

He started on another of his speeches about true fidelity, but Lynne came into the room, dressed like a bag lady in creased trousers and some kind of shapeless beige top. Stephen went back to his muesli.

Of course, when Juliet and Nigel turned up in response to one of Stephen's adverts and agreed to move in to the next door community house, Stephen was convinced that his focus had paid off. He was beside himself with delight.

Juliet was one of those small, delicate looking women. She reminded me of a willow sapling. She had pale skin and hair that defied description, something between red and gold. Everything about her was neat and precise. Nigel was one of those hearty rugby player types. He had high colouring and mousy hair that flopped in his face and made him look boyish, though he was in his early thirties. They joined us in October eighty-six. They had two little girls, Heloise, who was two and a half and Freya, who was just a couple of months old. Both of the girls were tiny and golden haired like Juliet.

Stephen was ecstatic about the children. He insisted I go to London to do the new Soulful Parenting workshops that Ralph and Annabel had launched. Of course I jumped at the chance. Ralph was as kind and gorgeous as ever. It did my soul no end of good to be affirmed by him.

Back in Bristol, I started to settle into my new role as Soul-Guide. I've always been good at sensing things. I soon realised that Nigel was in the same position as me. Stephen wasn't there for me and Juliet wasn't there for Nigel. She was so preoccupied with the girls and I hardly think they had sex at all after she got pregnant for the third time.

In a way Juliet was like Annabel. She had no understanding of true fidelity. I found her crying in her kitchen one morning. Her perfect skin blotched from weeping.

"Juliet, what on earth's wrong?" I glanced around her pristine lemon kitchen wondering if the children were still asleep. "Where are the children?"

Juliet sniffed and grabbed hold of a tea towel to wipe across her bloated face. "My friend Annette's got them."

"Annette?"

"She lives a few streets away. I met her at a playgroup."

"Juliet, I don't want to seem judgemental, but do you know this person well enough to entrust her with your little goddesses?"

Juliet glared at me and I noticed how unattractive her watery blue eyes looked, veined and bloodshot. "To be honest, Caro, I'd let the dustbin man look after them today." She breathed in deeply, choking back more tears.

"You really shouldn't hold your emotions in like that, you know," I warned her. "Do you want to talk about it?"

"Talk about what? Entrusting my kids to Annette or why I'm crying."

I smiled patiently, "Why you're crying, Juliet."

She looked at me as though she was about to blurt out something vicious, but only said quietly, "Nigel is having an affair."

"What?" A wave of nausea hit me. The yellow walls of Juliet's kitchen looked suddenly sickly.

"You heard right." Juliet pulled out a kitchen chair and slumped beside the table. I walked over and joined her, trying to quell my rising panic.

"How do you know?" I asked. I reached out a hand to her thin arm and kept my voice steady.

"He told me."

"Why? I mean why would he do that?" I stood up and almost tipped over my chair, but caught it and sat down quickly.

"I had my suspicions, so I asked him straight out. He's crap at lying and he knows it."

"But that's mad. I mean why would he..."

"Because I'm not enough for him, Caro." She looked so weary and small. I stood up and hugged her head into my belly. I stroked her shiny gold hair and thought how dry it was. She really needed to use a better conditioner.

Juliet looked up and forced a tired smile. "I'm not even thirty yet, Caro, and I'm already a boring old frump who only thinks about nappies and which coat to put on the girls when it's cold."

I sat back down and appraised her for a moment. She was hurt, bitter even, but she didn't seem to be angry with me. I tried to keep the quaver out of my voice, "Did Nigel say who he..."

Juliet anticipated the end, "Some nubile secretary at the bank. How clichéd is that?" She picked up the tea towel and, disgustingly, blew her nose on it.

"I suppose it's a cliché because it happens a lot." I said quietly, trying not to let my relief show. "You know, it probably doesn't mean anything, Juliet. Stephen always says fidelity is really..."

Juliet shot me another withering look and cut in, "That's bollocks, Caro. Sorry, but when it comes to these things I'm a conservative. All the soulful bullshit in the world won't convince me otherwise."

"Juliet!" It was my turn to be shocked and at least a little pleased that I could securely take the high ground now that she had challenged Soulful Living.

"Let's leave it, Caro." Her face looked less puffy now and her eyes only a little red. She had a way of making sadness and fatigue look appealing, I thought, a little envious of her delicate features. "I've asked Nigel to leave and he says he will. Apparently the bank has been pushing him to move for a promotion, but he didn't tell me. He didn't think I'd want to leave the community. He'll take the job and go. It's only in Swindon, so he can see the girls when he's not too busy with his fancy piece."

Juliet sighed heavily and stood up. I stood too. She embraced me suddenly, a fleeting gesture with no energy in it, and smiled wanly, "Annette's lovely, Caro. She has a little girl a few months younger than Freya, called

Genevieve. You'll like her. She'd love to learn about Soulful Parenting. Anyway, I need to go and rescue her from Heloise and Freya. Thanks for the shoulder."

It was a blow loosing Nigel, but Stephen was unperturbed. As long as we had Juliet and her girls he was more than happy. I wondered if he was sleeping with Juliet, but I could hear him tapping computer keys in the writing room whenever I woke at night. I was pretty sure that Nigel had been right about Juliet. She might be pretty, but she had no sex drive. Some women seem to give up on themselves when they have children. It took Nigel only a couple of months to move out. We stopped sleeping together in case Juliet discovered the truth. I wasn't ashamed, but clearly Juliet didn't have the soulfulness to understand and I didn't want to risk her leaving the community.

Annette started to come to Soulful Parenting gatherings not long after Juliet gave birth to Caitlin. Annette also brought her friend Sophie, a plump, short woman with bobbed brown hair and a loud laugh. They both had daughters, little goddess souls to join the community. Annette's daughter hardly looked like a Genevieve. She had the same dull, mousy hair as her mother. Sophie's little girl was a couple of months younger, a plump little toddler called Olivia. Neither of their husband's would come to classes with Stephen, but at least Annette's husband was less surly. I was as happy as Stephen to see the community growing. A year after Caitlin was born, Sophie gave birth to another little girl, Hannah, and the community finally seemed to be taking off.

"You know, Sophie is really making great progress." Stephen told me. "I'm so glad for her that she's had another girl. It'll make it much easier for her to bring up two little goddesses on the same path without the distraction of a little soul bringer."

Gradually more people came, but despite our successes, those were hard years for me. I was lonely with Nigel gone and I only managed occasional visits to London for Soulful Parenting workshops. Even when I was there, seeing Ralph was always marred by the suspicious looks and acerbic comments that Annabel would toss at me. We went on holiday and I managed a brief fling, but it couldn't satisfy me for long. I suppose I should be thankful that at least Stephen's holiday escapades prowling bars fired him up enough for him to get me pregnant.

Indigo and Xanthe were born on January 28th 1990. We planned a home birth so that every stage would be a perfect example of soulful birthing. But the doctors were unco-operative about allowing a home birth for twins and even the wonderful midwife that had delivered Juliet's Caitlin at home shook her head over me. We had to fight even to be allowed to let our babies go to term, but my waters broke a week early.

"I'll phone Sister Murphy," Juliet announced, "And an ambulance. A taxi might be a bit squeamish about…"

"No. Don't phone yet. It could be hours before the contractions speed up." Stephen had read everything about labour. A wave of pain hit me and I screamed, loudly. It doesn't do to hold these things in.

"I think we should call now. They can monitor the babies. I'm all for being as natural as possible, but twins are more complicated, Stephen."

I squatted onto the red floor cushion and then bent onto all fours.

"I want my babies born at home." Stephen said. His voice had a low menacing edge to it. "If we wait, it will be too late to move her. They'll have to do it here."

Juliet shot Stephen a look of pure hatred, but said, "Okay, Stephen. You're the father. I'll just pop next door and get a few things I used to make myself more comfortable when I had Caitlin."

Juliet went next door and phoned Sister Murphy. I suppose I'm glad she did. At least I didn't have to have a caesarean, which is the most unsoulful start in life that a child can have.

After the twins arrived I had some sympathy for Juliet's lack of sexual urges, but only for a couple of months. Goodness only knows how she could go so long. Juliet always told me how exhausting young children were and I could see what she meant. There were times when I thought I'd die of fatigue, especially on those days when Lynne had one of her selfish flounces and left me alone to struggle with two demanding babies. But really, women shouldn't use tiredness as an excuse to allow their souls to shut down. We owe it to our daughters to live fully as soulful people. Of course, that's easier said than done when you're living in an area apparently devoid of eligible men, have a husband with no interest and, worst of all, a body that feels suddenly alien. Leaking breasts and a stomach that sags are hardly turn-ons.

To make things worse, Stephen announced that I'd have to wait for the twins to be older before I could leave them to go to Soulful Parenting workshops in London. Ralph sent me his new books, which were starting to do well among a discerning group. But it was hardly compensation for being with my mentor in the flesh.

127

"Caro, I'm going to be out of the house today." Lynne announced after breakfast. It was one of those freezing March days. "You'll be fine with the twins, won't you?"

I was dumb-struck at the selfishness of the woman. I dissolved into tears. "Lynne, you can't go. I can't possibly cope with two ten week old babies for a whole day alone."

"Stephen's upstairs," she retorted coldly. She was wearing some kind of khaki coloured jumpsuit that made her bad skin look even worse. It crossed my mind to tell her that she would benefit from seeing the dentist about having her teeth whitened, but I was too shocked and upset to be helpful.

"You know Stephen is writing, Lynne. I need you here. You can't possibly expect me to cope alone. What about changing nappies?"

"It's not rocket science, Caro." I don't think I'd realised how cruel Lynne could be until that moment. "Even from the distance you watch from, you must have some idea of how to do it by now."

"But I might not get the folding right. What if they wriggle when I'm doing the pins? Anyway, you know I simply can't bear the smell of the bucket. I'll retch and be ill."

She eyed me without sympathy. "The nappies are already folded in the back room and if you're stuck you can send Stephen to the shop for some Pampers."

"Lynne! How could you even think I'd use those ecologically destructive things on my angels? They're full of poisons and besides…"

"Sorry, Caro, I have to go."

She actually walked out and left me to it. I sat and sobbed as quietly as I could, terrified that I'd wake the babies, both asleep on blankets surrounded by floor cushions. I willed Juliet to come in from next door, but she didn't appear. Instead there was a knock on the front door. I glanced at the babies, still asleep, and crept out into the passageway. When I'd quietly inched the door open, it was mousy Annette's husband, Dave, standing there.

"Dave. Hello, I didn't expect..."

"Are you alright, Caro?"

I'd always thought he was the most sensitive of the husbands, but I hadn't noticed before how tall Dave was, a head taller than me and in good shape too. He had rather limp hair, but sweet eyes, brown and lively. And his mouth showed kindness. I smiled at Dave and invited him in. Across the road I noticed the trees lining the park were budding. It would soon be spring after all.

Bethan turned up that summer and life blossomed even more. I still hankered for an occasional trip to London, but at least there was Dave, who turned out to be even more sensitive than I'd guessed, and a new member of the community, even if she did secretly eat meat.

It was five years before I visited London alone. Stephen made trips frequently and once or twice condescended to take me and the twins along. The trips were hardly relaxing, though. Lynne selfishly refused to come and help, insisting that she needed some 'down time', so I hardly got a moment alone with Ralph. If it hadn't been for Dave I don't think I would have survived those years. But it wasn't ideal. Dave was always at work or else Annette was around. What I needed was to come first with someone, but that never happened: not with Stephen or Ralph or Dave.

At home, Stephen hardly lifted a finger to help, and I was so busy with all the other parents in the community, looking to me to guide them. Sometimes I felt utterly overwhelmed.

I tried to make things better with Stephen from time to time, but that only led to his vile suggestion that I should dress up like a school girl. Then to find out that Stephen was sleeping with Lynne! At least Stephen had the decency to ask Lynne to leave. I couldn't have survived if he hadn't. Sleeping with Lynne was so much more humiliating for me than his little fixation on schoolgirls.

After that awful holiday with Bethan, Stephen never came to bed at night. The loneliness ate deeper and deeper. I felt I'd implode under the strain of it. The next two years were the worst years for me and Dave too. He wanted the fun, but he wasn't interested in my emotional needs. He whined about all the pressures on him. We saw each other less and less and when we did it often ended sourly.

Then I met Justin at a weekend Soulful Parenting gathering in London. I'd just finished a one to one guidance session with Ralph. He'd been patiently explaining how I must nurture each aspect of my soul. He went through each charka on my body, his hand resting on each site as he talked. His hand moved slowly down from my head, across my neck, breasts and abdomen. When he reached the base chakra I could feel the red energy surge through me, uniting body and soul as he moved his hand between the top of my thighs. I so desperately needed nurturing, but the door opened.

"Ah, there you both are." We both jumped at Annabel's crisp, cold voice. She shut the door behind her with a brisk click, while Ralph turned away quickly and fumbled with his zip. "Caro, dear, you looked terribly flushed. Are you feeling alright? Perhaps you should get some water," Annabel oozed.

"I... I'm fine, Annabel. Ralph was just finishing a session on chakras for me. I suppose I was just so wrapped up in what he was saying. I think I might go and get a drink." I tried to sound ordinary while my whole body buzzed with frustration.

"You do that dear. I know how intense these little talks of Ralph's can get." She smiled, but I could read the suspicion and jealousy in her aging face and cold green eyes.

I bumped into Justin outside Ralph's room. Justin began to talk about how much he cared about his little boy. He had a way of moving his strong, articulate hands as he spoke. I longed to pull him to me there and then, though of course I didn't. It was another three months before we even slept together.

Dear Ceridwen V

When Bryn phones I emerge from sleep like a diver surfacing cautiously. A knot of anxiety clutches my stomach before I remember that it is only five in the afternoon where he is. I can't remember my father's voice, but in my mind it merges with the sound of Bryn: smooth and rich like good port. Today, though there are pauses; air locks in his voice where he carefully stores away normal conversation for fear of upsetting me. He doesn't tell me how well Gethin is doing or gush about the mountains of Christmas baking Mary has already done.

In the morning the tree lights are slowly brightening and softening, the way I left them when I went to bed so that I wouldn't have to darken the room before I left it. I will force myself to do some shopping today. I know Dafydd's daughter Eleri would gladly shop for me; it would make her feel less guilty about enjoying her family Christmas if she could do something practical, but Nain goads me to shop for myself.

When I walk past the little park by the post office I see mothers nod towards me sorrowfully and look to their own children, suddenly fussing over a hat or glove or holding on to a child for a few seconds longer than they normally would.

I will shop to appease Nain's voice and because it would be terrible if you appeared on Christmas Day and there was no festive food to greet you. I'm not sure I can face a turkey. The sheer volume of the thing would reduce me to tears, but I will buy a duck, which you prefer anyway.

December 23rd 2003
Dear Ceridwen

The summer that Matt left for Newcastle I had a letter accepting my first poetry collection for publication. But the success seemed dull. Juliet, for all her criticisms about letting Matt go, was a good friend. She was constantly at my door offering to take you to the park, but even Juliet couldn't pull me out of the doldrums. It took another Christmas with Nain to bring me back to myself.

Soulful Parenting classes went on as ever. I noticed with horror that after Matt left you stopped objecting to staying over, though you always slept with Juliet's girls next door, never the twins. I remember that I asked you if Matt had ever hurt you, if you were ever frightened of him and you laughed at me.

"Matt!" Your eyes were fiery and incredulous. "Don't be so daft, Mum!"

"And everything's okay?"

"I'm fine, Mum. I miss Matt and Alicia."

"But everything else is okay?"

"I said I'm fine." Your tone and expression were resolute.

It was a spring day when I bumped into Caro out of her usual environment. I had arranged to borrow some books from a college in Redland for the refugee project. The trees fringing the Downs had small new leaves and sticky green buds; the sun was bright and even a little warm.

I loaded the books into my car and drove a little way down Whiteladies Road. I thought I'd buy vegetables for supper, stop in the art shop for the paint colours that you had mentioned you were running low on, and maybe take

133

some time out for a cappuccino. I wasn't sure of what I was seeing at first, but Caro was hard to miss. She had on her white silk trousers and a new tunic, a swirl of several shades of purple shot through with deeper purple threads. Her long blond hair hung straight to her waist like a curtain and she was holding hands with the man who walked beside her. From behind I didn't recognise him, except to be sure that it wasn't Stephen. He was taller than Caro and his hair was thick and curly.

They stopped and turned towards one another, embraced and kissed. I screwed my eyes up to focus on the man, trying to place him. It was Dave; Annette's husband Dave. Caro turned towards me as Dave walked away towards the college. I remembered he worked there as a technician. I ducked into the door of the art supply shop until Caro was almost level with me, then sauntered into her path.

Caro jumped. "Bethan!" She composed herself and hugged me to her, lavishly kissing my cheek as though she hadn't seen me in a long while. "What on earth are you doing up here? I thought your... your, er... centre was near St. Paul's?"

"I had to pick up some books from the college. That was Dave wasn't it?"

"Pardon? I'm not sure I'm following you, sweetie." Caro's voice was even, but her eyes darted up the street to make sure that Dave was out of sight.

"The man you kissed just now. That was Dave?"

Caro looked suddenly wan and vulnerable, her shoulders collapsed and a tear formed at the corner of one eye. "Sweetie, I can't tell you what it's been like for me. I know you'll understand."

"Do I want to understand? Dave's married. He's got a daughter. Annette's your friend. She comes to your parenting classes."

"Bethan, sweetie! You have to listen to me. Things are never as simple as you like to think. Sometimes you're so... well, so Welsh I suppose."

"What on earth's that supposed to mean?"

"Oh, sweetie, don't take offence like that. I only meant with all those chapels and everything... I mean I'm the first person to know how religion can screw you up, with the upbringing I had..."

"Caro, I've hardly ever been in a chapel in my life and I think we're getting off the subject."

"Right, well, all I meant was you mustn't judge. Dave and I, well we need things our partners can't give us, but we're not about to go breaking up any families and nor should you."

"How long have you...?"

Caro eyed me and put a hand on each of my shoulders, "You mustn't jump to any conclusions, sweetie. We've been... well, seeing each other for about ten years."

"Ten years?" My voice came out too loud so that a passing couple turned and glanced at us.

"Bethan, I'll tell you all about it, really I will. I'll come over tonight and we can share a bottle of wine when Ceridwen is in bed."

"Ceridwen doesn't go to bed till ten o'clock, Caro, she's thirteen. I'm asleep not long after her."

"Well when would be a good time then?"

"This weekend. Ceridwen is going to an art workshop with her friend Sana."

"Right. I'll ask Lynne to baby-sit. I'm sure that will be fine." I must have pulled a face at the mention of Lynne's name. "Really Bethan, I can see the judgement written all over you."

"I was just thinking that when you made all that fuss about Stephen and Lynne you must already have been seeing Dave for five years. I don't understand it, Caro."

"Well, I'm sure you will, Bethan. I'll see you on Saturday, about eleven."

Caro sailed away and I stood outside the art shop for a long time.

Saturday came, but Caro's life made no more sense to me. She told me that she'd started seeing Dave when the twins were a couple of months old. Stephen wasn't interested in sleeping with Caro and Dave was burdened with frumpy Annette. She'd had another affair before Dave, Caro confided, though she wouldn't tell me the first man's name. She told me that she and Stephen had always meant to have an open marriage and that she'd had a long term on and off relationship with her hero and guru, Ralph Goodman, whose books we followed religiously in Soulful Parenting classes.

"I'm sorry, Caro, I can't understand all this! If you and Stephen have such an open marriage, why were you upset about Lynne? You certainly made it seem like a big deal at the time."

"But Bethan, don't you see? It was Lynne! Stephen has a type, a kind of girl he likes in bed. I was forced to look elsewhere because he made it so clear that I wasn't his type, sexually, at least. He saw me as a mother to his children, but that's all. I had to come to terms with that, Bethan, but then to find out that he'd slept with Lynne. It was so insulting, Bethan. You must understand."

I shrugged. "So what are you going to do now?"

"About what?"

"God, Caro. I know. I know about you and Dave and I see Annette several times a week and Ceridwen is friends with Genevieve. What now? I don't want to feel implicated, but I do."

"Oh, sweetie, you're so black and white about everything, but if it will put your mind at rest I can stop seeing Dave."

"That easily?"

"Yes."

I looked doubtful.

"Really, Bethan. I hardly have much going on with Dave any more. It's all a bit stale to be honest and he's been getting uneasy for quite a while. It won't be any trouble to finish things. You're right. I can't ask you to compromise yourself. The thing is though..."

I held my breath for what would come next.

"I'm going to have to leave Stephen, too, but I don't know how. He's screwed up all the money his Dad gave him, so I won't get a penny, but I can't take much more. You don't really know him at all, Bethan."

I sat at my kitchen table, a small oblong of scrubbed pine scattered with the morning post, a plump tea pot filled with fruit tea for Caro and my newly acquired spun steel cafetiere and said nothing. Across the table Caro sipped at dark red tea and watched me.

"I can't come to any more classes." I said eventually.

"But, sweetie..." Caro began, but fell silent. She put her mug down and waited.

"How can I learn better parenting from people whose lives are such a mess?"

"I think that's a bit harsh," Caro said quietly, not meeting my gaze, "Soulful Parenting is an ideal we all work towards. We don't have to be perfect."

"Perhaps, but I can't come anymore, not to groups."

"You won't stop Ceridwen from seeing the children?"

"No, why should I?"

Caro looked relieved, "Indigo is so in awe of Ceridwen's artwork. She loves having an older friend to look up to."

"This is nothing to do with the children and I didn't say I'd stop coming, but just not to groups. I don't think I can keep those up with Annette sitting there soaking it all up like a sponge."

"I understand." Caro stood up, carried her mug over to the sink and walked out into the hallway. She turned before she reached the front door. "I really have to leave Stephen, Bethan. He's killing me, sucking the soul out of me. I don't know who I am when I'm with him."

Caro didn't leave Stephen, not then anyway, but she became more erratic.

"Last night she burst into tears twice in the gathering – in the middle of sentences," Juliet sighed, "I'm sure she's having some kind of breakdown, but she won't talk to me."

I nodded and sipped the coffee that Juliet had started to buy openly, despite the protests from her house-mate, Rachel.

"Last week she suddenly announced that Stephen was keeping her prisoner. Then she laughed it off a minute later. Attendance is getting a bit erratic, I can tell you that," Juliet added. We were sitting in her neat, pale living room listening to the vibrations of music that came from Heloise's room overhead. "Rachel is totally freaked. She told me she thinks she might look for somewhere else for her and Lucy to live. All I can say is you bailed in very good time, Bethan. Did you have forewarning?"

"Not exactly."

"But you knew something was up?"

"It's kind of confidential, Juliet."

"Hmm. You know what I think? I think Caro has got someone else. She keeps talking about leaving and she wouldn't do that unless she had some other man to lean on. Am I right?"

"Juliet, you're terrible. It's confidential."

"Ah, so I'm right. Caro's had affairs before you know."

"What?" I sat forward uncomfortably, wondering how much everyone knew. Was I the only one never to suspect these things?

"She had a thing with my ex husband."

"No!" I elongated the word and shook my head. "When?"

"That's what broke us up. I didn't know at the time or I'd have left here long ago. Nigel told me a couple of months ago in one of his morose remorseful moods. At the time he told me it was a secretary, but he made that up to cover for Caro."

"Have you told Caro you know about it?"

"I don't see the point really. It's an old wound. He's been gone thirteen years nearly. I was pregnant with Caitlin. Anyway, the state Caro's in right now I'd probably end up feeling like a bitch for making her cry."

So that was the name Caro wouldn't tell me, I thought.

"I'll tell you what else I've noticed." Juliet went on, "Those two haven't been throwing money around as though it were confetti recently. There's more up the creak than their love life."

"I think you're right about that, but I don't know the details. To be honest, I'm not sure if even Caro knows the

139

details. I think Stephen keeps her in the dark about money."

"And keeps her prisoner?"

"I think she wants to leave, Juliet, but the money is a problem. I don't know how he could actually stop her though."

"She's not just cracking up in front of the group, Bethan. I have this friend, Philippa, who works at the community centre. She hardly knows Caro, but she told me that Caro came in for some photocopying and started telling everyone there how she is a prisoner in her own home and needs help. Then she burst into tears all over the place. Poor Philippa hadn't a clue what to say."

"Maybe you're right about a break down?"

"I think she's right on the edge, Bethan."

A few days later Stephen paid one of his occasional visits. We sat at my table, just as I had with Caro, the same pot of fruit tea, the same jug of coffee, a slightly hotter Saturday in late June.

"I'm really grateful to Ceridwen for taking Indigo along to the art workshop today, Bethan."

"It was no trouble. They have the same tastes and Indi's very grown up for her age. Ceridwen says she's cool."

Stephen smiled his thin, pensive smile that never showed teeth. "I worry more about Xanthe. She's so much more volatile. I'm afraid she reminds me of Caro and I'm anxious for her."

"Anxious for Xanthe or Caro?" I asked

"Honestly? Both of them. You know I'm not one for doctors, Bethan, but I think Caro needs to see someone."

"You know she wants to leave you, Stephen?"

140

"I know she says she does, but she's really not my prisoner. Not that I want her to go. She's the mother of my children, for God-sake, and I can't think of anything worse for them than us splitting up. The thing is, I don't think she's herself at all. It's not just the crying. She's going up to strangers in the street telling them she's a prisoner and that I'm psychically abusing her. I have no idea what she's going to say or do next. Sooner or later she's going to do something serious, hurt herself or say something so frightening that someone will call social services."

"Social services?"

Stephen shifted uneasily and pushed a hand through his thinning hair. "Well, people might think she's not a fit mother or might be dangerous for the children."

"But Caro's never violent, Stephen."

"Of course I don't think she'd ever hurt the children, but if you met a mad woman in the street who accused her husband of all kinds of weird stuff and then claimed to be his prisoner, wouldn't you think of calling someone?"

"I suppose I might," I agreed.

"She needs proper help, but anything I suggest is taken as an attack." He put his head in his hands briefly, then fixed my gaze. "I mentioned seeing a doctor a couple of days ago and she got absolutely hysterical. She started throwing things and saying I was trying to brain wash her into believing she was insane. She even told Rachel that I'm tying to have her committed. I daren't speak to her again. I don't want to push her over the edge." His voice cracked as he finished.

"And that's where I come in?"

Stephen put his hand on my arm. "I know it's a lot to ask, but I trust you and Caro does too."

"I don't know how I'd even begin."

"I know, I can understand that, but you're my only hope. I don't think Caro could hurt the children no matter what, but I'm worried she might try suicide or something. When she's worked up it's like she's another person."

"I can try to talk to her about getting some help, but it's up to Caro whether she stays or goes, that's not my business."

"I understand, but you don't really think she'd be better off without me do you? She isn't emotionally strong enough to look after the girls alone and they need their home."

Stephen withdrew his hand from my arm and watched my face intently. He went on, "I know about the affairs, Bethan. She's seeing a man called Justin at the moment, someone she met at Soulful Parenting workshops in London." He spoke quietly, gazing into his mug of tepid fruit tea.

I think that was the first time I felt any tenderness towards Stephen. He had always seemed so aloof, so devoid of emotion, but at that moment I wanted to wrap him in fluffy blankets, like a little boy with flu.

"I'm sorry. I didn't realise."

"She tells me about her affairs to hurt me. I know I haven't always been all that she wanted. The thing is, there's a part of Caro that could be easily bought off, a few romantic gestures, little gifts and shoddy flowers, talking to her like she's a brain dead bimbo. I know I could do those things and compete with any man in her life, but I don't want to stoop to that. I never have. I've always wanted something more real and grown up between us, but I suppose I should have compromised more."

I gulped coffee while he paused for breath. He had me riveted to every word.

"Justin is good at the showy stuff, but that's all. He'll hurt her when he's bored, but I'll still be here. I don't even mind. If she really needs a string of Justins in her life then so be it. I just want us to be open with each other and keep a stable home for the girls. I can't bear to think of them being dragged through their parents' divorce, the sordid pettiness of it all and then having two homes, whatever that's supposed to mean. I blame myself, Bethan, I really do. I should have been more attentive, more romantic, more anything she wanted. I'll do anything it takes to make her happy again. I just want the Caro I've always loved."

Stephen put his head into his hands and his shoulders twitched slightly, enough to reveal that he was softly crying.

I bought the whole story. Despite all of Caro's infidelities, which seemed to make the incident with Lynne fade into insignificance, he was a man still in love with his wife, desperately trying to shield his daughters from divorce and from their mother's breakdown. Even so, words always failed me whenever I tried to talk to Caro about seeing a doctor.

Instead, I began house hunting, not in Easton or Eastville, but further away, across the motorway in St. Werburgh's. The house I found was similar to the one we rented. My new job was more secure and Bryn had been telling me for years that rent money was wasted money. You were excited about decorating a new room and the bus journey to school was only slightly different. Juliet came and cried over my kitchen table, but I told her the extra walk would do her good. We weren't moving far.

Lynne, who had been invited back the previous autumn when Caro seemed to be breaking apart, arrived with Stephen while I was packing. It was a hot June day, much hotter than the day a year earlier when Stephen had sat at my kitchen table and poured his heart out. They hovered while I taped and marked the last boxes.

"Bethan, I know the decision is made, but I needed to tell you that I'm very disappointed in you," Stephen launched in.

I stood up from the box I'd just taped, a roll of brown tape stretched between my hands, the sweat of packing and lifting making a damp pool at the back of my white t-shirt. "I'm sorry, Stephen, what on earth are you talking about?"

"With all that's happening right now, the last thing Caro needs is for you to up sticks. She trusts you. She needs you round the corner. And in any case, all this scurrying after property and material security; it's hardly soulful."

I stared at Stephen for a while, wondering why I'd felt so much sympathy, even tenderness, for him in the last year. "Don't be so bloody pompous, Stephen." I leant over the next box, listening to Lynne's shocked intake of breath as I scrawled 'KITCHEN' on its side.

"Bethan, this is immoral, what you're doing. I don't just mean trying to buy security for yourself rather than trusting the Universe to provide, that's bad enough, but this desertion. You're leaving the community and that's a hostile act at a time of crisis. You are thinking of no-one but yourself."

I straightened again and smiled. "Stephen, be a dear and piss off."

144

I wandered upstairs to direct the removers, not looking back to see how long Stephen and Lynne stood in my almost emptied downstairs.

From the landing I heard Lynne say to Stephen, "You can't trust her, Stephen, not any more. She could ruin everything."

Caro V

The truth is that Bethan is the one who can't be trusted. She doesn't think twice about betraying people; just look at how easily she gave up on Matt. Bethan was the first person I turned to when things were bad between me and Stephen. She heard all that crap Stephen spouted about fidelity not being anything to do with who he shagged. She knew exactly what he was like. She knew Stephen never made love to me. I even told her what he'd said about wanting school girls. Well, perhaps I told her the school girl thing after Ceridwen had accused Stephen of… It's hard to hold all these things straight in my mind. It's all become so confused. What I do know is that I was the one who was abused by Stephen for years. It's hardly surprising if I can't quite remember exactly what I told Bethan or when I told her things. The point is, I did tell her. If anyone's in denial it's her.

At the trial even the judge commented on how Stephen had corrupted our home. He should have added that I was the real victim. Children are so resilient. I was the one who Stephen brain washed and manipulated more than anyone.

I definitely told Bethan that the only thing that would make Stephen shag Lynne was if he was being blackmailed by the poisonous frumpy toad. Of course Bethan didn't take the hint. I even told her straight out that Stephen was worried about going to prison, but she made some stupid remark about Stephen fiddling his taxes. I suppose I may have talked about how Stephen was up to his neck in fraud, but all she had to do was read between the lines. I don't believe she wanted to know the truth.

She was just as stupid over Matt. She fell for Stephen's story so easily. One minute she was in love with Matt and the next she was giving him the cold shoulder. Even Juliet was disgusted with Bethan about that. As if Matt would ever hurt Ceridwen or his precious Alicia, the most spoilt child I've ever met. The twins found it awfully hard to live with her, especially Xanthe, and they're so easy-going.

The last year with Stephen was the worst time.

"I want to leave. You can't stop me."

"Of course I can't, Caro." He stood in front of the bedroom door, blocking my way. His hair was un-brushed and he had a grease stain on his linen shirt.

I slumped on the lavender patchwork quilt. I loved it so much when I bought it, but now everything in the bedroom was tainted with Stephen. Nothing in that house was mine. It was all I could do to talk through my sobs.

"All I'm asking is that you calm down, Caro. You can't make decisions like this. You're overwrought." He moved forwards to hold me, but I flinched away. He put a hand on my shoulder and I tried to shake him off, but he kept hold.

"Look at you, Caro. As if I would ever do anything to hurt you." The blue of his eyes looked even more piercing than usual. I could smell sour sweat on his palm.

I sucked in a sob. "I know my own mind Stephen. I'm not mad."

"No one is saying you are mad, Caro. What I am saying is that you need to take some time, get some perspective, not rush into anything."

The tears howled out of me. Through the blur of wet salt and mucous I could see the way his bottom lip curled in distaste.

147

"Caro, if you would just see someone. I don't think you're mad, but I do think you're stressed. It might help to have someone to talk things through with, that's all I'm saying."

"No!" I tried to jerk his hand away, but still he gripped.

"Caro, if you go to the doctor yourself everything will be fine. Lots of people need to see someone from time to time. But frankly Caro," he put both hands on my shoulders, his eyes narrowed, "if you don't see someone and things get worse I'll have no alternative... I'll have to go to the doctor myself. I'm not saying they'll commit you, but you never know how these people might see things. I mean with the way you've been approaching strangers in the street, saying all kinds of wild things, they might think it best if you weren't around the children. You do understand, don't you?"

I pushed him away and screamed. I wasn't crying anymore. I was screeching the way I imagined I would if a stranger in an alley had me cornered. Stephen slapped me hard so that I felt the bone in my cheek vibrate with pain. The skin of my face burned. He smiled that thin-lipped, satisfied smile. He put his hands back on my shoulders and clamped harder.

"You're not helping yourself. Maybe I was too optimistic about you seeing sense. Maybe having you committed is the only way. Of course, I'll have to tell them there is mental illness in your family. The whole sordid story about your Daddy the Archdeacon and how he ended his days a broken, drooling alcoholic will all have to be dredged up again. Then there are all those depressions your lesbian mother went through. They'll need to know the full picture to be able to help you, Caro." He spoke slowly, watching my face.

148

"You can't! They wouldn't believe you!"

"Wouldn't believe what? Your family history is all on record isn't it? And you... well, look where you where when I found you – in a hostel after escaping your violent boyfriend, the one after the one who'd got you pregnant at seventeen. Then there's the affairs. And everyone thinks you're having a breakdown? Every shop assistant on Trinity Street knows you as the mad crying woman."

"I'll tell them! I'll tell them everything about you!"

"Really? More wild stories from the loony lady? You open your mouth and you'll never see the outside world again." He let go of me with a final shake.

I collapsed on the bed. My cries wrenched every fibre of my body. The tears and mucous flooded through the patchwork. Behind me Stephen leaned forward and began to stroke my back.

"It doesn't have to be like this. You can have your freedom. You can screw Justin and Ralph and every man you meet for all I care." He paused to pull my hair back from my face and smooth it down my back. "All I ask is that you don't jeopardise the community any further. You give me what I want and everything will be fine. The girls will still have a stable home, the community can go on as always and you can live your own sordid little life. Everyone wins, Caro. Surely that's what you want?"

I didn't answer. I continued wailing until I was too drained to make a sound. My body felt bruised inside by the continual jolt of tears. Stephen stood over me until I was still.

"Just think about seeing someone. And try to control yourself in public," he said. The quiet menace in his voice made me shiver. I heard the door click open and close again as he left.

I trusted Bethan with everything. When she moved house, I took her a tiny jar of frankincense and a little brass incense burner. She had painted the living room in a thick cream colour with one long wall in rich Victorian red. The futon was covered with a dark red cotton throw that Ceridwen had stencilled with gold stars and bronze moons. There were new cushions on the red horse-hair sofa, squares of dusty red and plum velvet. The kitchen and dining room were knocked into one with an L-shape of cream units around two walls and her scrubbed pine table and two newly acquired second-hand armchairs by the gas fire. Between the chairs Ceridwen had suspended a mobile she'd made out of bark, shells and feathers. Under the stairs, Bethan had fitted her Welsh dresser, scattered with her best mugs and plates.

"You've made it very homely already." I smiled, offering my parcel, "A little house-warming gift. It's not much."

"Thank you. Come and sit down." Bethan looked at me as though she was anxious about something. We sat in the armchairs and she unwrapped the parcel carefully, smoothing the blue tissue paper as she went.

"Ceridwen will use the tissue for something, no doubt." She peeled back the last thin layer, "Oh, Caro, it's lovely."

"It reminded me of a tiny thurible, the incense burners n churches. I used to be the thurifer at my Dad's church when I was little, when it all seemed like nice fairy stories and my Mum was still with us."

"You mean the person who swings the incense? I've seen it on TV, but I always thought it was a Catholic thing."

"High church Anglicans too; Anglo-Catholic. When I was really small I was the boat girl. I carried this little Aladdin's lamp shaped thing full of the incense and had to hand it to the thurifer on a long brass spoon. This burner just reminded me. I should have got some charcoal with it. Sorry."

"No, it's lovely. I'm sure Ceridwen's got charcoal. She burns incense in her room, but not in anything this lovely. Thank you, Caro. Can I get you a drink?"

Bethan made drinks and pulled up a little table between us to balance them on.

"Stephen came to see you didn't he?" I launched in as soon as Bethan was sitting opposite me again.

"A couple of times." She looked strained again.

"About me?"

"Well, last time he came to tell me how immoral I was for moving away from the community. I don't usually tell people to piss off, but I was in the middle of the move."

"And the other time?"

"He was worried about you. He wanted me to ask you to see someone, but I never felt like it was my place."

"He says he's going to have me committed."

She leant towards me. "He couldn't possibly. I'm sure you have to be a danger to yourself or others for that."

"He knows things, Bethan. My family weren't exactly normal." I could feel the tears, but tried to hold them back.

"Your Dad was an Archdeacon, right?" Bethan put her drink down and spoke softly, concentrating on me. She had on ear-rings that I hadn't seen before, silver loops hung with thin wires that ended in tiny amethysts.

"My father had a breakdown," I told her, biting back the tears. "He drank himself into it and then he drank himself to death. Before that he used to beat me and before that my mother ran away with her lesbian lover."

I paused for Bethan to take it all in and sipped my fruit tea. Bethan had new mugs as well as a new house and decorations. "My mother's still alive, but I don't see her

151

much. She's alone now and she gets these really bad depressions. She's just too hard to be with."

Bethan stayed quiet and nodded occasionally.

"Anyway, Stephen says loads of people think I'm mad because I'm always crying and telling people he holds me prisoner. But he does. It's the truth."

"I know Stephen can be pretty convincing. He made me feel sorry for him not so long ago, but I really don't think anyone would stand by and let him make you look insane. If you really want to leave, you've got to go for it."

"Really?" I was so grateful to Bethan.

"Really, Caro."

"The thing is, I do feel sort of all over the place," I confided. "I'd like to go to my doctor and get some counselling, but I'm frightened he'll use it against me."

"Well maybe that's the best thing you could do. See your doctor and arrange to see a counsellor. People don't have to be insane to visit a doctor with problems. Having a professional on your side might not be a bad thing."

"You think?" I felt the brightest I'd felt for months. I sipped more fruit tea and admired the cobalt blue mug. Bethan always had good taste.

Later, when Ceridwen and the others started making accusations, I couldn't have been more helpful. I told Bethan all about Stephen's obsession with Ceridwen, how he'd cried over her and how he was never in my bed at night. I trusted her with everything.

Bethan wasn't the only who let me down. Lynne came back to live with us not long after Bethan saw me with Dave on Whiteladies Road. In a way I was glad to have Lynne back. At least I didn't have to worry about cleaning the place or cooking meals anymore. She knew Stephen liked everything tidy, not that he ever lifted a finger to make it happen. And Xanthe and Indigo adored Lynne.

Lynne still made puppy dog eyes at Stephen, but anyone could see he was never going to shag her again. She had the kind of skin that wrinkles young and she'd aged a lot in five years. She was dowdier than ever and looked more like mid fifties than mid forties. I think she'd put on weight too. She certainly had no idea what she looked like from behind in those shapeless overalls.

Lynne loved being back. She took to lecturing me on how I should behave with the children; on how I should conduct myself in public; on how I should be more loyal to Stephen and the community. It felt like being back at home with my dad. I was always a disappointment.

The days when I had been away from home were always the worst. I'd walk in to be greeted by music so loud that my throat vibrated. It wasn't like my own home at all. I'd stand in the hallway, exhausted from the horrid train journey back from London and already missing Justin. I'd open the living room door a crack and hear a communal whine from inside.

"Caro! Before you start complaining, the children are having fun," Lynne hissed, coming to the door so that I couldn't get into the room.

"Don't be such a spoil sport, Mum." I heard Xanthe say.

"Oh, Mum!" Indigo added wearily. "Go and run yourself a nice bath."

One day I peered round the door to see Stephen standing behind Freya, his hands over hers, pulling her to him as she danced. In front of them Indigo, Lucy and Genevieve had collapsed in a giggling heap. They were all in a state of half-dress.

"What kind of dancing is this, exactly?"

"Don't be so disparaging, Caro," Lynne snapped. "It's just a bit of fun."

"It's called go-go dancing, Mum." Xanthe added.

Since Lynne had come back, Xanthe always seemed to have a scowl in her voice when she talked to me. The other girls laughed louder and rolled on the cushions like lion cubs at play, cute and sharp toothed.

I edged out of the room and Lynne followed me. "Caro, you need to be more supportive of the children. You know they are everything to Stephen."

"It depends what you mean by everything." I shot back.

"Don't be vulgar, Caro, it's unsoulful. Everything he does is for their needs. Children need to explore things without being judged, you of all people should know that."

"I'm sorry." I backed away from Lynne's onion breath, crept upstairs and began making calls to estate agents.

When the truth came spilling out like guts from a knife wound, it was Lynne who scared me most. I went round to talk to Stephen, but Lynne wouldn't leave his side. When I left, she followed me out into the hallway. "If you say one word against Stephen we'll bring you down with us," she hissed.

I stared at her, dumb-founded and shocked. I noticed her mousy hair was turning grey at the temples.

"Do you understand?" Lynne persisted and I nodded. "And on no account are those precious girls to be handed over to the police. Filth isn't a strong enough word for those people. If you let them near your girls they will fill them with shame. They'll be damaged forever."

I nodded again and made for the front door.

Dear Ceridwen VI

I wake up crying. My pillow is soaked with tears. I wander into the bathroom and notice how the light through the windows looks different, more yellow than usual: snow. I remember how much you wished for snow every Christmas that we spent here and my tears begin again. I sit on the bathroom floor and howl, grateful for the two foot granite walls and lack of neighbours. I howl for the sheer physical loss of you, the dark curls that are so like mine, but are not mine; their smell already fading from my memory, something like coconut and lime, but different. How does it smell? What is the precise tang and odour? I jump up, hunt through the bathroom cabinet, but there is no leftover bottle of your favourite shampoo, and if there was it wouldn't be the same, cold and glutinous in a plastic bottle. I slump down onto the toilet seat, defeated.

Nain always made scotch pancakes for breakfast on Christmas Eve, but downstairs I can't so much as summon the energy to light the fire, let alone force myself to mix batter or go through the motion of a ritual that will only remind me that you are absent. Outside the kitchen window I glimpse the garden running down to the stream. For a moment I almost conjure you. The last time it snowed heavily Bryn, Mary and Gethin were visiting. You were twelve and Gethin was seventeen. He was as patient as ever with you, making snow men and snow angels at the bottom of the sloping garden.

'You can't invoke the living, girl,' Nain says beside me. 'She's not dead, cariad. You just have to wait for her.'

"It's too hard, Nain. I don't think I can stay sane much longer."

'I'm not saying it's easy; howl at the moon if you need to, but don't stop eating, girl. You have to keep body and soul together for when she comes back, Bethan. And keep writing that book for her. She'll like that. Have you got her something to put under the tree?'

I collapse onto the little sofa under the window and cry some more.

When the sobs die down Nain's voice is soft, her milk at bedtime voice, 'There now. You just have to go on putting one foot in front of the other, girl.'

I sniff and nod, unconvinced.

'For a start you need to get that stove going, and the one in the living room too. I can't abide a cold house, never could.' She is brisk again, sharp sun on cold snow. 'You want to get those fires going before the stones chill. Once this granite takes in the cold it's a devil to heat through again, you know that well enough, girl.'

I rouse myself, fetch coal and light the fires.

December 24th 2003, Christmas Eve
Dear Ceridwen,

Caro left Stephen a few months after we moved house. She hated her rented house in Easton, a two bedroom terrace in need of decoration, but she was proud that she had made the move. After Caro moved, she started talking openly about her relationship with Justin.

"Xanthe says her mum is a slut," you told me one morning while we were getting breakfast.

"That's pretty strong language for a not quite eleven-year old to be using."

"Sheesh, Mum, they learn it all at school. There are six year olds who shout worse things than that in the playground."

"Nice," I offered, grimacing, "how about Indigo?"

"She's not saying much, you know Indi, but I think she's pretty cut up about the whole thing. Xanthe says no way is she sleeping or eating at Caro's place."

"That's going to be hard for them to sort out. What does Stephen say?"

"Haven't a clue. I've got to go now, Mum."

Xanthe was as good as her word. Caro complained to Juliet that how badly Xanthe behaved towards her, but it didn't stop as Caro enjoying her new found freedom. She visited Justin whenever she had the opportunity and soon he began to visit her in Bristol. Xanthe was so irate with the new arrangement that she stepped up her campaign and refused to go to Caro's house at all.

"Caro was really drunk again last night, Mum," you told me one Sunday morning after you had slept over with Indi. You scooped your curls into a red hair band and twisted it into a rough bun at the back of your neck. "I'm going to get a long bath. Caro's place is a bit... well, filthy really. When she got drunk she started crying about how Lynne never comes round to clean for her. Sheesh."

"Did you eat?"

"I took Indi out for chips. She's not really allowed them, but we were starving after the art workshop and Caro's kitchen's a mess."

"Maybe you and Indi would be better off staying here or at Stephen's place." I suggested.

"Caro likes Indi to stay with her. I have to get a bath now Mum."

Sometimes you stayed at Stephen's, though only when Caro was away in London. I invited you both to stay with me of course, but Indi was nervous of other people's houses and no doubt she had heard Stephen's speeches about how I had betrayed the community by moving a couple of miles away. Juliet was even more protective than me about her daughters spending time with Caro, even though Heloise was sixteen by then. Both of us whispered anxiously about whether Caro should be left alone with children. We worried that she might get so drunk that she could harm herself or even one of you. Of course, neither of us worried about you staying with Stephen or about Juliet's children sleeping in their own home where Stephen had complete access. Instead, Juliet and I urged you to stay clear of Caro as though we were being responsible parents. The more dishevelled and dysfunctional Caro's life became the more we felt sorry for Stephen.

"Mum, could Indi borrow some money for today's art workshop?"

It was February, a couple of weeks after the twins twelfth birthday, which both Stephen and Caro had celebrated in the most cursory way.

"Of course she can, did she leave her money at home?"

We were standing in the hallway just outside the living room where Indi was sitting waiting for you. You grabbed my arm and marched me into the kitchen.

"Don't let Indi hear you, Mum. Caro and Stephen are broke. They had an awful Christmas and Caro took the CD players she bought for the twin's birthday back to the shop."

"So when you say borrow?"

You flashed a winning smile, "I might mean could you pay for us both for a few weeks."

"I see."

"I'd feel awful if she couldn't come with me, Mum."

"Do Caro and Stephen know I'm paying?"

"God knows, they don't know what day of the week it is, let alone what their kids are doing."

"Ceridwen, I really don't think it's a good idea for you to sleep over at Caro's while things are so…" I searched for a diplomatic word, "unsettled. I presume Stephen still has food in his house and doesn't get drunk"

"Yeah, like Stephen would drink. Lynne has food in the house, but we're okay at Caro's. Indi likes getting chips."

"Ceridwen, I'm not happy…"

"Whatever, Mum, can I have that money? We need to be going."

Caro paid me a visit a few days later. Her skin looked grey. There was a small red stain on her lavender tunic and her normally pristine silk trousers were crumpled.

"Can I have some coffee?" Caro asked in a small voice. She spoke without moving and looked smaller without her usual expansive gestures.

"Of course, come and sit in the kitchen."

Caro slumped into one of the blue fireside armchairs and sank her head into her hands so that her hair fell forward, not in its usual sleek curtain, but in greasy folds.

I busied myself with the kettle and coffee grinder.

"There you go. Are you alright?" I tried to sound cheerful as I held out the blue mug.

"Not really. Do you have any idea how demeaning it is claiming benefits?"

"I'm afraid I don't."

Caro sipped her coffee and closed her eyes for a few moments. "I hate that house I'm reduced to living in. It has a smell. Like old people died there, nasty old people. I think it might be haunted as well as tasteless."

I started to laugh despite myself, but managed to suck down the snort. I could see from Caro's eyes that this was no laughing matter.

"Stephen won't give me a penny. He's says he's hardly got any money. He says I spent it all on trips to London and clothes and holidays and goodness knows what else. I don't see how it's even possible to spend that much money. It'll all come out in the divorce, but he won't answer my solicitor's letters. He says it's unsoulful to be a party to breaking apart the girls' home; their bloody 'soul-sanctuary' he calls it."

Caro spoke quickly, gulped down coffee and pushed back a tangle of hair. Her eyes were deep sunk and red-rimmed.

"It'll take ages to get a divorce if he won't sign anything and he'll use up all the money that's left while he keeps me dangling. He's such a bastard, Bethan."

"I'm sorry things are so awful," I said lamely. "Maybe you should spend the time while you're waiting for the divorce taking care of yourself. Get yourself back together, ready to start a new life with the girls."

"What's that supposed to mean?" Caro slammed her mug onto the little coffee table so that coffee spurted over the rim.

"I only meant I'm worried about you. Are you eating properly?" The bones on her face jutted out, so that she looked skeletal rather than slim and statuesque.

"What you really mean is am I feeding the twins properly and am I drinking?"

160

"I was asking about you, but if you want Xanthe to come round to staying at your house, it has to be welcoming. They need somewhere where they feel looked after."

Caro began to weep.

"Xanthe hates me. He's made her hate me. He's made her believe I'm an insane slut. If Ceridwen didn't make Indigo come round to my house I'd hardly see her either. She only comes out of pity."

The sobs crescendoed. She wiped mucus on her sleeve and continued to howl.

I squatted on the floor beside Caro's chair and laid a hand on her leg. "I'm sure Indi wants to see you. I know it's hard, but the more she feels it's homely the more she'll be comfortable there. Xanthe will come round. You're her mam, no matter how confused she's feeling. She still loves you."

Caro sniffed loudly. "Ceridwen likes it at mine best."

I nodded, appeasing her.

"Ceridwen is such a sweetie. She cleaned up my kitchen last Saturday evening when Lynne hadn't turned up to help again. Ceridwen's a real goddess. She's got more sense than to hang around bloody Stephen's place!"

I flexed from the cramped position I'd been in and sat back in the armchair opposite Caro.

"Maybe it's best if the children don't have to choose sides, Caro?"

"At least I wouldn't hurt her."

"Hurt her? What do you mean? "

For a reply, Caro covered her face with her hands and sobbed some more, but quietly this time, like someone choking in the distance.

"I get these ideas, Bethan. I've been telling my counsellor about them. I have these terrible panics when I think

Stephen will go mad and murder everyone or do terrible things. It's the stress. That's what my counsellor says. "

She reached for her mug to finish the coffee.

"Do you think Stephen's attractive, Bethan?"

The question seemed out of the blue.

"Well, not really. He's kind of…" I searched for the right word, "bland I suppose; neutral."

"No vibe?"

"Exactly."

Caro nodded. "All he cares about is the girls. That's all he's ever cared about."

I laughed uneasily. "I should talk. I'm not exactly out there myself. I suppose some of us just don't have the same kind of…"

"Sex drive?"

I didn't answer.

"Maybe some people have a different sort of sex drive," Caro said. She straightened and looked more like her old self for an instant.

"I'm sorry… you've lost me."

"Well in Stephen's case let's just say 'wanker'." Caro grinned and put down her empty mug. "Thanks for the coffee, Bethan."

By summer Caro seemed more herself. She still complained bitterly about her awful house and the lack of money, but the drinking slowed down after Ralph invited her to lead some Soulful Parenting workshops in London. She was even more cheered when Justin's decree absolute came through in July and he acquired a London flat that was sumptuous even for her tastes. She was still bone thin, but she bought new clothes; tight jeans decorated with hippy embroidery to replace her floaty tunics and flowing silk trousers, high heeled boots instead of espadrilles.

We went to Tŷ Gurig half way through August, staying longer in Bristol that summer so that you could take part in a community art project. I knew as soon as we arrived that Nain was ill, or perhaps more accurately that she was fading. It seems ridiculous to most people that anyone would be surprised to see the life leaking out of a ninety-two year old woman. Afterwards we heard all the platitudes about how she had a good innings, but we were still caught off balance; winded by the physical loss of someone who seemed eternal.

I was grateful for Dafydd after the funeral service; he sidled over to me awkwardly and said, "I'm sorry about Megan, cariad, untimely it was."

I had to force my brain to remember that Nain had a name. Megan. Dafydd was talking about Nain and he was right, to us it would always be untimely. I nodded and squeezed his arm and slipped out into the garden, down to the river, where Bryn was already pacing. We held each other and I cried for the first time since Nain had died. The last time I'd cried on Bryn I was five and he was seventeen and we'd just lost our parents.

You seemed distant from me that autumn. I could see you going through the motions at school, doing what you needed to do to scrape by. You lost interest in the community art workshops and I told myself it was the loss of Nain, that doing art was too painful because it reminded you too much of all the things she had taught you.

Caro was away a lot that autumn. In London she could dazzle new young parents with her soulful knowledge of the mysteries of childhood and bask in their admiration. You stayed at Juliet's house whenever Indigo begged you to have sleepovers with her. I noticed your mood darkening as Christmas approached and thought you were grief stricken, that you were brooding about our first Christmas without Nain.

"I know it's awful, cariad, but we have to decide what to do about Christmas."

You looked at me as though I was from another planet and I felt my guts twist with your loss, with what I thought you were struggling with.

"We can stay here if you want." I paused, speaking slowly, as though grief might make it harder for you to understand sentences. "But I was thinking that in a way that might be worse. We'd be thinking about Nain and Tŷ Gurig anyway, so perhaps we'd be better off facing the place. And I don't like to leave it empty all the time, even with Dafydd keeping an eye on things." You looked back at me, but your eyes were dull and tired. "What do you think, love?"

You stood up and shook yourself, a small shiver of the kind that would make Nain say someone had walked over your grave.

"Whatever you like, Mum, I don't really care about Christmas."

I thought you meant you were missing Nain too much.

It was a year ago today when you told me. Here in this room where I am sitting next to a tree with no presents under it besides a fire that has no power to reach the cold in me. Christmas Eve, after we'd decorated the tree that Dafydd had brought the day before. We laid our gifts under the tree and sat on the sofa to admire it.

You said, "I can't go to Stephen's house any more, Mum."

"Oh dear, cariad. You haven't fallen out with Indi?" I twisted to face you and you ducked your head down.

"No. Xanthe gets on my nerves, but she doesn't bug me that much. It's not that."

"So what's the problem?"

There was a long pause. You looked at me for a while, your eyes ringed in dark shadows.

"Stephen."

I waited for what felt like an age and watched you colour slowly, the pink flushing through your cheeks before a single tear appeared.

"Ceridwen?" My throat was dry.

"Stephen's a pervert, Mum. I can't take it any more!"

You fled from the room. I heard you run upstairs and turn on music, something loud that made the granite stones of the house vibrate, but even the music couldn't mask the banshee howls that were coming from you.

That was our longest night together. Years of torment poured from you in one long storm. I rocked you as I had when you were a baby, but I had never heard you cry like that. It was five in the morning before we slept, slumped awkwardly together on your bed. We woke only a few hours later, stiff, aching and changed.

You smiled at me, bravely. "Happy Christmas, Mum."

I stroked your hair, which was matted where salty tears had dried onto it from the sodden pillow.

"I'll be all right now," you said quietly in a voice like Nain's.

On the day of the interviews we sat in the artificially pristine house used by the police. Juliet and I made tense, synthetic conversation as though we were strangers waiting for root canal work without anaesthetic. They took you in order of age: Freya, you and Caitlin. Afterwards, the fourteen hour ordeal of that day became known amongst us as 'the special day out', a kind of ironic humour to remind each other of what we had survived. In the next days and weeks more girls told their stories. When Caro refused to let Indigo and Xanthe speak to the police it was you who made the first stand.

"I'm not seeing Indigo any more, Mum."

"Are you sure?"

"Positive. I know it's Caro stopping her talking and maybe she really didn't know anything, but Xanthe did. Freya said Xanthe knew stuff and I believe Freya. It's too hard to see them, Mum, all of them. Caro and Xanthe and Indigo. Everyone else is in this together and I can't stand the way they act like it's nothing to do with them. Caro was there. She was always there, Mum."

The day before Stephen was sentenced you disappeared. Do you know that he was sentenced to seven years, Ceridwen? The girl from the Probation Service told me he will be able to apply for probation after he's only served half of it: Christmas 2006. She was a pretty, fair-haired girl in her early twenties.

"It's better that he serves those last fourteen months in the community where he can be supervised and receive treatment. We can keep an eye on him and help him to address his offending behaviour."

I wanted to scream at her that 'offending behaviour' was not like a wart that could be cured, but I only refilled her coffee cup and smiled.

I miss you so much, Ceridwen. I wish I knew that you were safe.

Caro VI

Stephen would have ruined my life if I'd let him, but I found my strong place after all. We're doing well now, me and Xanthe and Indigo; incredibly well. Tomorrow it will be Christmas Day and the girls will wake up in Justin's gorgeous apartment and unwrap all the presents I've been able to buy them now that I have a job. It's important to give them treats after all we've been through this year. In the New Year we'll go back to Bristol and move into our new house in Montpelier, so much nicer than grotty Eastville. Lynne has taken over the house I rented in Easton, gradually getting the place decorated, but she's promised to be available for childcare. I know what she's up to, milking the children for information about my life, passing on messages to Stephen when she makes her sordid prison visits. Still, what else can I do? I have to have someone to help me now that I'm a single working mother.

Justin did ask me to move in with him. I was tempted, especially when Ralph offered me a full time post in London with the Soulful Living Foundation, as it's called now. It's all very exciting now that they've got charitable status and some kind of government money to teach parents from poor areas how to play with their children. It was very kind of Ralph to offer, but it was time to move on. I have to have my own space for now.

It was ironic that it was Pam the social worker who got me the interview for my new job. I didn't really take to her at first. I suppose it's only natural to think that fat people are likely to be a bit stupid and lazy and we did get off to a bad start. She was so taken in by everything Juliet and Bethan said about me and I'll never quite forgive her for insisting I tell my poor darlings why their father was arrested. Still, it turned out that there was more to fat Pam than her weight. Once she'd heard my story she completely understood. It was good of her to think of me when this charity sent her details of a post for someone to co-ordinate their outreach work to mothers of abused children. Pam knew that I had a lot of experience working with parents and she said my name just sprang to mind. With a recommendation from Pam and Ralph's reference, I really couldn't fail to get the job.

When I look back it's amazing that I've turned my life around so completely in only a year. I'm sure it's the Universe's way of affirming my innocence. I deserve good things. I'm not saying that I don't feel sorry for Bethan, I do, incredibly sorry that she's had to give up her job and crawl back to that place in Wales in the middle of nowhere, all alone, not even knowing where Ceridwen is or whether she's alive. I have this awful feeling that if she's not dead she's hanging out with druggies and prostitutes. It's terribly sad, but what goes around comes around.

Things weren't easy with Xanthe, not for a long time. It's only natural that a little girl doesn't want to believe bad things about her own father. I understand that, but she had to be made to understand that her father is a complete bastard and that I was the victim in all of this.

At first she soaked up all the terrible things people like Bethan and Juliet said about me, but as time went on she heard a few home truths about Stephen. I could see by the way she watched me that she was revising her opinions of her precious father. She wrote as much in her journal, covering a whole page with 'I hate my Dad' scrawled at every angle, the words criss-crossing each other and making a hole in the paper. It's not something I approve of normally, reading someone else's journal, but as her mother I had to know what was going on in her head at such a terrible time.

Xanthe was with me in the kitchen one day when Dave came storming round. It took Genevieve a good two months after Ceridwen and the others started pouring out their stories to admit that Stephen had touched her. I can't imagine what Stephen saw in her. At fifteen she was already as frumpy as her mother, but I suppose all Stephen cared about was their age.

When the argument between me and Dave subsided, Xanthe stepped towards me. She ignored Dave and looked me in the face. Her own face was flushed to the roots of and her eyes looked a little bloodshot.

"You've been sleeping with Dave, haven't you Mum?"

I saw Dave flinch, but Xanthe had her back to him.

"Darling! Wherever do you get these ideas? Dave is Genevieve's Daddy and Annette's my friend."

"No-one's your friend, Mum." Xanthe rounded on Dave. "Get out and leave us alone or I'll tell your ugly wife what you've been doing."

Dave opened his mouth to speak, but instead he turned to walk out. He stopped at the front door and called back down the passageway, "Don't you come near me or my family again, Caroline Beaumont, you or your brats."

He slammed the door and I moved towards Xanthe, "Thank you, sweetie," I said, making to hug her, but she pulled away.

"Leave me alone you slut!" She shouted. She ran from the kitchen and up the stairs.

It was like that with Xanthe until Justin came to stay at Easter time. She threatened to run away if I invited Justin to stay in the house, but my instinct told me she was bluffing and I was right. It was Xanthe who opened the door when Justin arrived. She stood there, blocking his path while Indigo and I hovered behind her.

"Xanthe, sweetie, let Justin in and then I can introduce us all properly."

"No need for introductions, Mum." Xanthe stepped back and Justin hauled his case over the step and straightened. He smiled at me and my girls, about to say something, but Xanthe got in first. "I can tell who he is by the smell, he smells of you, Mum: eau de slut."

"Xanthe! Justin, I'm so sorry. She's had such a hard…"

Justin smiled at me unruffled, "Don't apologise for her, Caro. I'm sure Xanthe is quite capable of doing that for herself. I think we should have a little talk, young lady."

Justin took hold of Xanthe's arm before she could run to her room and propelled her into the living room, clicking the door shut behind the two of them.

Indigo looked tearful and shaken, but I couldn't help thinking that it was about time someone stood up for me. The air needed clearing.

"It's alright, Indigo. Justin is a skilled psychologist. I think perhaps it will do Xanthe good to have a little chat with him."

Indigo sniffed back her tears. She looked anxious, but she nodded bravely.

"We'll go and make drinks for everyone." I longed to listen at the door, but I had to keep Indigo occupied. I heard Xanthe begin to cry as I walked to the kitchen and was glad that Indigo had gone ahead of me. It would do Xanthe good to vent her feelings with someone else.

If I'm honest, the rest of Justin's visit was a little stiff. It reminded me of one of those evenings when my mother and father would entertain the Bishop and his wife and I'd be wheeled out to make polite, awkward conversation about how much I enjoyed school and what I wanted to be when I grew up. Still, it did make things better in the long run. Justin promised me he hadn't laid a finger on Xanthe, but he let her know that if it came to it he wouldn't be afraid to discipline her. No-one had ever spoken to her like that, but it did the trick. At least she started acting the part of a civilised person again and I'm sure she adores Justin now. She's always quiet around him and she hasn't called me names since that day.

I changed the girls' school at Easter. It was hard on them to move schools mid-term, but thirteen isn't such a terrible age to make a change. At least they've got each other. They couldn't go to the small school anymore with none of their friends speaking to them and I couldn't bear the thought of one of those awful state schools.

I hit on the idea of writing to the bishop in my Father's old diocese. I poured out my awful story of how I'd ended up married to an abusive man and now my innocent children were being ostracised in the only school they'd ever known. When I went to meet him I thought he was a bit cold at first.

"The thing is, Mrs. Beaumont, the church doesn't have money the way it used to. The school fees you're asking for are really more than we can..."

We were sitting in a twenty foot reception room furnished with Georgian furniture and it wasn't reproduction. The plush green carpet looked new and the wallpaper beneath the perfectly painted dado rails was at least *Sanderson*.

"My father used to abuse me," I said.

"I beg your pardon, Mrs. Beaumont?" He blinked stupidly and moved uneasily in his velvet upholstered arm chair.

"I had an abortion when I was not quite seventeen." I didn't mention that my father had nothing to do with the baby, or at least that his only part in it was in driving me away from home with his beatings. I watched the bishop's eyes widen and his face begin to take on the same colour as his magenta cassock.

"Mrs. Beaumont, may I call you Caroline? Caroline I…"

"He died an alcoholic, my father. I suppose it was guilt for what he'd done to me." I saw him open his mouth, but I kept talking, determined not to let him interrupt. "The thing is, now it feels like history is repeating itself. My husband turned out to be an abuser and I'm left destitute with these two innocent girls. I have to find the school fees from somewhere and the only other way I can think of raising the money is to do some interviews with the media. I can't talk about my husband's case, of course, the courts don't allow that, but there's nothing to stop me saying something about what happened to me as a child…"

He stood up and began to pace, "Caroline, I'm sure we can find some way to help…" He sat down and leant towards me as though we were old friends. "There is one charity I know of that might be just what we're looking for. I'll give them a call today."

I had a letter agreeing to pay the girls' school fees by the end of the week. I hated begging for charity, but it was justice to get something back form the church and proof that the Universe really does look after us.

I'm not saying that my life is perfect. Sometimes I worry about the twins. Xanthe's school reports aren't as good as

I'd like. It was embarrassing when she had that period of suspension before Christmas. I felt like a naughty schoolgirl myself when I was called in to see the Head Teacher and I had to be careful of what I said. I don't want him writing to the charity that pays the twins' fees.

I don't like the friends Xanthe hangs around with from Easton, people she met when she was staying over at Lynne's. They're a rough crowd, scruffy and fowl mouthed and it bothers me a bit that Xanthe calls one of them her boyfriend; a scrawny, acne covered boy of seventeen. I do wonder if that might be a bit old for a girl who's not fourteen till next month. I worry about what a bad influence they are, but, on the other hand, it's probably all part of growing up. I can't protect my angels from everything.

Indigo is the complete opposite, but I'm not sure she's made any new friends at school. She's very conscientious about her school work, though, and such a quiet girl.

I have to stop myself from being an over-anxious mother. I've always cared too much. I suppose most mothers wouldn't even notice these things. Really the twins are doing fine, and I shouldn't fret so much.

The twins are fine and I have Justin. We've been together for six years now, but I do think he's let things get into a bit of a rut recently. He's not as romantic as he was and it's important for me to know that I'm still beautiful and desirable. There's this guy who comes in to do counselling sessions with the women at the project where I work. MOACh, Mothers of Abused Children. He always flirts or passes some comment and it does me good to be noticed.

I've put a lot of work into my new look. I don't wear those awful hippy clothes anymore. I've got good suits in expensive fabrics with short skirts that show off my long legs and three different pairs of boots, making up for all the years when Stephen wouldn't let me buy leather. All my blouses are silk, white or pale colours that suit my colouring. I wear my hair pulled back, with a smart abalone clip over the hair band.

A couple of years ago I would never have believed that things could work out so well for me.

Dear Ceridwen VII

I wake stiff and cold. The cover on your bed has slipped off in the night and the clock tells me it's past ten in the morning. The light straining through your thin red curtains has a translucent quality; more snow. I force my limbs to move. On the landing Daisy mews at me and begins to head downstairs. She turns half way down the first flight, stares at me accusingly and mews again.

"Sorry, Daisy, is breakfast late today?"

I'm grateful for the excuse she gives me to talk out loud to something solid. I pad downstairs after her, snatching my dressing gown from the hook outside my room, and obediently scrape chunks of *Whiskas* into her bowl, refill her water dish and pour her biscuits. I pour orange juice for myself and take the glass back to the bathroom. I need the comfort of hot water before I do anything else today. I lie in the steaming foam and resolve to write more of your journal. I haven't been able to face it for the last two days, Christmas Day and Boxing Day, but they are over now and I want to finish.

After breakfast, I settle on my bed. The stoves are both unlit and the stones of the house are cooling, but I want to write. At my side are a tin of chocolates that Dafydd's Eleri brought on Christmas Eve, a whole carton of fresh orange juice and a hot cafetiere of coffee. I turn on the hardly used storage heater, flicking the over-ride button to allow it to gobble up expensive day time electricity, and open the journal.

December 27th 2003
Dear Ceridwen

It was hard letting you go the night before the trial, but I was so wary of upsetting you. It seemed reasonable that you would want to spend the night with Juliet's girls, especially since you had made plans to go with them and Juliet to the court the next day.

I waited for Juliet to phone from the court all day. It was about three-thirty when the phone finally rang.

"Seven years." Juliet sounded jubilant and tearful.

"Seven?"

"Yep. I don't know what the bastard will actually serve, but his face when they said it... Well, it was one of the more satisfying moments of this year, let's put it that way."

"Is Ceridwen alright? Can I speak to her?"

"Speak to her?" Juliet sounded bemused.

"Yes. Is she alright after being in court? Were Heloise and Freya okay?"

Juliet's voice dipped, "Ceridwen didn't come with us, Bethan."

"She decided not to?"

"Yes. She phoned yesterday to let me know."

I felt my guts churn. "But she did stay with you last night?" My voice sounded scratched and thin.

I knew the answer from Juliet's pause, "No."

"Oh, God."

"Bethan, don't panic. She might have gone to another friend. Maybe she decided to sit it out with Genevieve or Olivia. Neither of them wanted to be in court. Rachel and Lucy are here with me, so she's not with them. You ring Annette. I'll ring Sophie and Paula. What about her school friends? Maybe she wanted to be with someone who doesn't know about all this. Maybe she needed a break. Try Nisha and Sana's mums." Juliet gushed out instructions in a breathless stream.

I nodded at the phone.

"Bethan, are you still there? Are you alright to phone people?" Juliet's voice was calmer, more deliberate.

I nodded again, but managed a choked, "Yes."

"It'll be alright. Ceridwen's an amazing girl. It's just been so hard on them all."

I put down the phone and started phoning your friends. I tried Nisha and Sana's homes first, trying to sound nonchalant or at least ordinary. I was less held together with Annette.

"Thanks for letting me know the pig got seven years and I hope you find Ceridwen soon. I'm sure she'll be fine. She's a really special girl."

The phone rang almost as soon as I finished talking to Annette.

"Any luck?" I knew from Juliet's question that she hadn't found you with Sophie or Paula. "Well she's not with bloody Caro. The bitch was in court with Lynne. They left in tears of course." Juliet stopped abruptly, "God, Bethan, what next?"

"I don't know. Police?"

I heard Juliet strangle a sob. "Perhaps you should. Do you have a direct line for Gwen? I know she's a child protection officer, but she knows Ceridwen."

"Yes."

"Phone her now. I'll be with you as soon as I can. Try not to worry. I'm sure she'll be fine. I'm sure she… I'll be there soon."

That was more than six months ago. In the first week the police were back and forth to see me. Gwen brought a colleague I hadn't met before, an Inspector called Kevin Travers, who was adept at using several sentences to not answer my questions. After two weeks I phoned the missing person's helpline. I was give a key worker, Sue, who collected information about you, asked for recent photographs, told me that I could ring her anytime and hoped beyond hope for me when I was too disheartened to keep hoping for myself.

I panicked when the summer holidays came, wondering if you would come home to St. Werburgh's or head for Tŷ Gurig. I was terrified that I would make the wrong decision; that you would arrive at one house or the other, decide that I wasn't waiting for you and go away forever.

"Go home," Juliet said. "To Wales I mean."

I was a hard person to befriend in those months, I reminded my friends of their own dark fears. I was brittle and closed, but Juliet persevered. "You always say you're going home when you go to Wales, even after thirteen years here. Maybe Ceridwen feels like that too. There's plenty of people here who can let her know where you are if… Well, I'd go to Wales if it were me."

"Go back to Tŷ Gurig," Bryn said three nights in row on the phone. He and Mary phoned nightly, struggling to find the words to fill the space between us.

At weekends Gethin phoned too, a young man of twenty now, studying physics with the same intent seriousness his father had for literature and his mother for medicine. Gethin talked about you more easily than the adults, reminded me of the snow angels and the endless pictures you made him draw.

178

"Ceridwen doesn't do anything without a reason, Aunt Bethan, she's a real smart kid." He repeated that line with every call.

I came to Tŷ Gurig for the summer and haunted the place like a lost soul. I lost whole days sitting by the river remembering you and the tears finally came, sparked by random artefacts that took me unawares: a scratch on the kitchen table where you had slipped chiselling into a lino tile when Nain was teaching you to print; a chipped cup that Nain had put to the back of the cupboard rather than throw out because you had bought it for her as a Christmas gift when you were only four; a cardigan that you had worn to death when you were about twelve and that had fallen down behind the hot water pipes in the airing cupboard. These things ambushed me.

I wanted to stay at Tŷ Gurig, but I forced myself back to Bristol in time for the new term. Perhaps you would return to discover how well you'd done in your GCSEs, seven of them grade As. Maybe you would be back to take up your place to study A levels at sixth form: Art and English and French. I went back to work, but my heart was not in it. As the weeks slid away into long wet autumn days hope dripped away and fatigue set in.

I worked my notice in October, though I was absent for more days than I managed to put in. Juliet came to see me off, her face tear-streaked before she arrived. Annette and Dave had decided to separate as soon as the case was over and Annette and Genevieve moved into our house. It was a relief not to have to worry about how I would pay the mortgage without my job, more of a relief that if you turned up in Bristol it would not be a stranger answering the door, looking at you blankly or abruptly telling you the Prichards didn't live here any more.

I've been here a little over two months, Ceridwen, and still I am ambushed by small reminders of you on a daily basis. For the first month I had only Daisy to talk to, but Nain appeared in December. Perhaps 'appeared' is not the right word, but I hear her and sometimes I have an almost physical sense of her beside me. I imagine her hand on my head or my shoulder. Is it imagination? Nain tells me that you are not dead, but I still carry around this weight that is like sacks of sharp edged slate; the weight of your absence. I stay away from the river in case the weight overbalances me into the water and I drown clinging to it.

At night the weight of grief rolls onto my chest so that I struggle to breathe and have to sit up suddenly, panting. I talk myself into gulping down air. When you were born, I remember someone told me that sometimes newborn babies forget to breathe, that babies have to learn to keep making the right movements, in and out, in and out. This person, I can't recall who, told me that if I slept with you, you would keep breathing, that you would learn from me. At night, I'm like a baby who hasn't learnt to breathe and is left alone.

I look like a normal person; I walk, talk, comb my hair, and get dressed. I don't smell, hot baths being my drug of choice. My weight never seems to vary, whether I binge on chocolate or live on toast for a week. Only my eyes look different to me, older, more tired, always slightly red rimmed and dull, or the set of my shoulders, the tension that would be imperceptible to anyone but you. I wonder if the police thought I was a cold person; I didn't cry in front of them.

They told me that your file will remain open, but they have given up actively searching for you. Children go missing all the time, apparently, just like adults; twelve year olds walk out of their lives and into anonymity as if they had disappeared into a parallel universe. There are posters with your picture pasted around Bristol and London. They plead with you to simply ring home, but perhaps you wouldn't recognise yourself in images half scratched off lamp posts or rain-sodden.

What I want to write today is that I love you, Ceridwen. It is the only part of me not drained. My hope comes and goes. My faith in others has diminished; all the well meaning police and help lines in the world will not bring you home, I tell myself. But my love is resilient. Even in those moments of sheer rage when I scream and rant at you for leaving. This is what I want you to know: that I love you, I love you, I love you.

The bedroom is hot when I finish. The electric-guzzling heater smells of old dust and dry skin. I switch it off. I will light the living room fire, cook something warm for dinner and have a bath when the stove has heated the water.

Downstairs the tree looks sad; the needles are beginning to dull from the heat of the fire, even though I've stood it on the far side of the front door where it can breathe the draught. I flick the switch to give it tiny twinkling lights and move to pull the heavy curtains shut. Something catches my eye. On the mat in front of the door is a letter. I've forgotten that there is post today. The envelope is white, thick and good quality, written in a hand I think I've seen before. The post-mark is from Newcastle. Inside are two letters. I seize on the one in the handwriting I recognise immediately.

Dear Mam,

I'm sorry this is a letter. I know I should ring, but I think if I heard your voice all I'd do is cry down the phone. Matt wanted to ring you himself, but I've begged him not to and I wouldn't tell him the number. I wanted you to read my letter before anything else, so please don't blame Matt.

I'm not sure what happened that day before Stephen's trial. I intended to go to the court with Juliet, Freya and Caitlin, but I suddenly had this urge to be somewhere else, somewhere far away from it all. I knew Stephen would be sent to prison. I didn't know how long it would be for, but I knew it would be long enough to shock the smugness out of him. I wanted to see him get sent to prison, but I suddenly couldn't face being there. I think I was also worried about what it would be like afterwards. I thought everyone would be celebrating Stephen's sentence, but I'd know that it wasn't over for me. I wasn't ready for people to pat me on the back and say I could move on now.

Do you remember that night when I first told you? It was Christmas Eve at Nain's house, the Christmas after Nain died. I think I told you then because Nain wasn't there to hear it anymore. I couldn't have coped with her knowing what he'd done to me. Do you remember how I cried all night? I had a sore throat the next morning and I was frightened I'd ruined Christmas, but I was glad you knew at last. Do you remember 'the special day out' when we spent all day getting ready for the taped interviews and sat in that weird tidy house that was supposed to put us at ease? I hated that day, but it was a big release. I didn't feel like that when I knew Stephen was going to be sentenced. I felt sick thinking about what would be said in court. I didn't want to hear it all again or see the expression on his face.

I know I could have told you all that and just stayed at home. I know none of that probably explains why I ran away, but it didn't feel like I was running away. I felt like I was looking for something I'd lost. I'll sound like Caro if I say something corny like 'I had to find myself', but I suppose that's the nearest I can get.

The thing is, Mam, Stephen had been hurting me for so long, since I was such a little girl. I needed to see who I was apart from all of it. It felt so urgent, the most urgent thing ever. It blotted out every other thought. Once I'd left, I knew you would be going through a nightmare. I did care, really I did, but I knew if I got in touch I wouldn't be able to stay away. I hope you'll forgive me for that, even if I can't explain it properly.

I went to London first. I've never been interested in my dad but I think I had this idea that Stephen wouldn't have been able to hurt me if I'd had my own dad. I don't think that's really true. Quite few of the girls at the community had dads and that didn't stop Stephen. What I did find out was that my dad's got this whole other family. They have a house in London and another one in Gloucestershire. His kids go to private schools and his wife looks bored and sad. I think he's having an affair with his secretary. I didn't introduce myself and I'm glad we didn't end up with that life.

After London I moved around. I wasn't alone. I joined up with a girl called Tabitha and some New Age travellers. They were really cool people. You'd like them. They didn't ask me any questions. I needed time to think or cry or write or draw with no one asking me how I was doing. I hope that doesn't sound horrible. I know you have to worry about me, but I knew I couldn't bear it. I had to sort things out in my own head without feeling I had to put on a brave face when I wanted to scream or that I had to look upset when I was feeling okay. I don't think I'm explaining this very well.

The travellers went to this site in South Wales at the end of October. They use land that this eco-community own and there were some really cool people there, but after a while I knew I was ready to move on again. There was something at the back of my mind that was bothering me, and then it occurred to me. In all this time and with the police running round getting evidence by the bucket load no one had ever thought about Alicia. She was ten and half when her and Matt moved away and all I knew was that Matt had gone to Newcastle. I was lucky they were in the phone book. Anyway, I'll let Matt tell you about him and Alicia, but I was right about her, and Matt has been great.

I'm really sorry about missing the start of term. I wasn't ready for all the people and questions. To be honest, I'm not keen to go back to Bristol at all, but I know you have to work and our house is there. I'd really like to stay at Tŷ Gurig and I told Matt to send our letters there. I was sure you would be home for Christmas, even without Nain or me. If we can't live at Tŷ Gurig Matt says I can stay with him and Alicia. I could go to sixth form here next September, perhaps.

Matt will put his phone number on his letter and I can't wait to hear your voice, but I'm scared too. I hope you understand.

Heaps and heaps of love,
Ceridwen

I read your letter again, one fat tear-drop smudging your love at the bottom of the page.

'There now, girl, I told you she was alive, didn't I?'

I nod and the tears come thick and fast.

'Come on with you, girl, I want to know what Matt's got to say for himself before the year turns.'

I wipe my eyes and smooth out Matt's letter.

Dear Bethan,

I can't believe it's more than six years since we last spoke. Ceridwen has turned into a young woman to be reckoned with and I didn't need to look twice to see whose daughter she is. Alicia will be seventeen next March and she looks more and more like Elaine every day.

First of all, a million apologies for not contacting you sooner. I know I could have found your phone number without too much problem, but Ceridwen was adamant that she wasn't ready and she desperately wanted to contact you herself once you were at your gran's house in Wales. If I was in your position I'm not sure I could forgive anyone who kept quiet about Alicia's whereabouts for a second, but, in my defence, I was worried that Ceridwen would leave us if I did anything to pre-empt her.

Secondly, I'm really sorry to hear that your gran died. She was a pretty special lady, not to mention the best cook I've ever met. Alicia and I still talk about that wonderful Christmas we all spent at Tŷ Gurig.

When I left Bristol I hadn't a clue why everything had fallen apart on me. Like everyone else, I suppose I didn't imagine Stephen capable of those things in my wildest dreams. All I knew was that one minute I was trying to look after my little girl, fearing she might have a kidney problem, and the next minute I was under suspicion and being interrogated. When I look back with hindsight and with what Alicia and Ceridwen have told me, I can piece it together. I can only assume that Stephen was setting me up; he must have imagined that he could make me the fall guy.

Alicia didn't have anything wrong with her kidneys. Stephen was abusing her just like all the others. Apparently one day Xanthe walked in and saw something and later told Alicia she was a 'disgusting slut'. Nice talk for a child of seven, but none of us realised what kind of environment those poor girls were growing up in. It was after that Alicia's nightmares and bed-wetting started and I suppose Stephen thought Alicia might make an allegation, so he wanted to point the finger at me first. I'm not sure how that would have helped him if Alicia had spoken up. Maybe Stephen and I would have both gone down, but he certainly wasn't going down alone and he managed to get rid of us both, so Alicia wasn't a weak link anymore.

When we left I decided not to keep in touch with anyone. I didn't know what Stephen had done to Alicia, but I felt raw about things and I wanted a fresh start for us. I know Juliet was really upset that I didn't want to stay in contact, but it seemed the best for everyone at the time. Of course it meant we were in the dark about all that you've been going through this year.

Alicia hasn't decided what to do next. With Stephen in prison any charges she brings will be separate, but my guess is that even if he pleads guilty the sentence will run concurrently. I'm going to get some legal advice on that, but frankly, Alicia seems to be thinking it's not worth going through the trauma of an investigation unless it will keep the creep locked up a bit longer.

It has been incredible to watch these two girls helping each other so much. Alicia has been a much quieter, more timid person since we left Bristol. There was always something held back in her and I put it down to her losing her mother and then losing you, her chance to have another mum with a sister thrown in.

The girls have spent a lot of time locked away in Alicia's room, talking and talking. Sometimes I hear crying or hysterical giggling and it's all I can do not to run in, but I've respected their privacy and it's been worth it. I can visibly see Alicia getting lighter everyday.

I know Ceridwen has mentioned staying here and I don't know how you will feel about that. You must ache to have her back with you and I think she knows that, but the thought of Bristol seems too overwhelming for her. Anyway, phone soon and we can talk about the future. I'm sure we can sort things out and Ceridwen isn't the only one who can't wait to hear your voice.

All my love,
Matt

When I phone the ringer hardly sounds before the receiver is lifted. We both rush to speak at once. I begin to cry and laugh at once.

Jan Fortune-Wood is an educationalist, poet, novelist and editor. Her previous publications include several books, chapters and articles on education and parenting, the most recent being *Winning Parent, Winning Child* (Cinnamon, 2005); a novel, *A Good Life* (Bluechrome Publishing, 2005) and collection of poetry, *Particles of Life* (Bluechrome Publishing, 2005). She lives in North Wales with her husband and children and is currently learning Welsh.

Cinnamon Press
Independent Innovative International

Cinnamon Press Writing Awards:

Four writing competitions with two deadlines each year for: Debut Novel; First Poetry Collection; Novella; Short Story

Deadlines June 30th and November 30th

All entries by post + sae & details - name, address, email, working title, nom de plume.

Novel: 1st prize - £500 + publishing contract. Submit 10,000 words. 5 finalists submit full novel & receive appraisal. Fee: £20 per novel.

Poetry Collection: 1st prize - £100 & contract. Runners up published in anthology. Submit 10 poems up to 40 lines. Three finalists submit further 10 poems. Fee: £16 per collection, includes copy of winners' anthology.

Novella: 1st prize - £200 + contract (20 – 45,000 words). Submit 10,000 words. Four finalists submit full novella. Fee: £16 per novella.

Short Story: 1st prize - £100 & publication. 10 runners up stories' published in winners' anthology. Length 2,000 – 4,000 words. Fee: £16 per story, includes winners' anthology.

Entries to: Meirion House, Glan yr afon, Tanygrisiau, Blaenau Ffestiniog, Gwynedd, LL41 3SU. Full details:

www.cinnamonpress.com

Z608638